Some other books by Robert Leeson

In Puffin

THE DOG WHO CHANGED THE WORLD
TOM'S PRIVATE WAR

For younger readers

NEVER KISS FROGS!
GERALDINE GETS LUCKY

PUFFIN BOOKS

Liar

Robert Leeson was born in Cheshire in 1928. He served in the
Army in the Middle East and worked abroad before returning to
Britain, where he has been a journalist for over forty years. He is
the author of sixty books for young people, as well as studies of
industrial history and literary criticism for adults. In 1985 he was
awarded the Eleanor Farjeon Award for services to children and
literature. Robert Leeson is married with a son and daughter, and
now lives in Hertfordshire.

LIAR

ROBERT LEESON

PUFFIN BOOKS

PUFFIN BOOKS

Published by the Penguin Group
Penguin Books Ltd, 27 Wrights Lane, London w8 5tz, England
Penguin Putnam Inc., 375 Hudson Street, New York, New York 10014, USA
Penguin Books Australia Ltd, Ringwood, Victoria, Australia
Penguin Books Canada Ltd, 10 Alcorn Avenue, Toronto, Ontario, Canada m4v 3b2
Penguin Books (NZ) Ltd, Private Bag 102902, NSMC, Auckland, New Zealand

Penguin Books Ltd, Registered Offices: Harmondsworth, Middlesex, England

First published 1999
1 3 5 7 9 10 8 6 4 2

Set in 11.5/13.9pt Monotype Bembo
Typeset by Rowland Phototypesetting Ltd,
Bury St Edmunds, Suffolk
Printed in England by Clays Ltd, St Ives plc

British Library Cataloguing in Publication Data
A CIP catalogue record for this book is available from the British Library

ISBN 0-141-30143-0

One

If I'd remembered things in a different order, what would have happened to Tel? Would he have still been alive today?

Right now I wouldn't even be able to remember all that I remembered, if I hadn't written it down – in between looking for Tel. *That* I did do – look for him, though I didn't understand why at the time, 'cause I was following a trail of the lies he'd told, all over the place, when the real truth was a lot nearer. But I did look for him, when some people didn't understand, and some didn't care, and one did worse.

It wasn't my idea to write it down, though. That was Mr Robinson's. Just before term end he said: Take a big sheet of paper and divide it in two. On one side write down happenings from your past life. On the other side write down what made you remember them.

At first I didn't do anything. Well, I drew a line down the middle of this sheet of paper and left it for a few days. Then I wrote 'Past' on one side and 'Present' on the other, and that's as far as I got.

Nothing strange in that really. Nobody takes holiday assignments seriously. And I do have this problem with getting started. I can do nothing for long stretches at a time. My mates are always banging on about being bored with nothing to do, but I can't see the problem.

At first I couldn't remember anything from the past. It's like my mind is a long corridor with doors. The more I try the handles, the more the doors stay shut. And that gets worse at exam times; the whole corridor closes down.

Tel never had that trouble.

He could remember everything – well, everything they wanted him to remember. In exams he'd finish first, then look round with a little smile on his face, then hand in his paper while we all watched him.

That smile is on his face in a passport photo he gave me just before term end, when he told me he was going off on this world tour. He signed it: See ya. Tel.

Don't try too hard, Mr Robinson told us. Memory can't be forced. Just let it come, then write it down, as you remember. So that's what I've been doing, writing things down as I remember them, in that order.

What you need, said Mr Robinson, is a stimulus. The mob at the back started laughing and nudging. But Robinson took no notice. He gets the time-wasters, the drop-outs, the under-achievers who aren't into serious A-levels, the ones with no chance in the job market. That was the strange part of it; how, after all, Tel landed up with us.

Mr Robinson looked over our heads: 'What you need is a trigger.' Then he rambled on, his eyes shining, about a French geezer, dead years ago. He was having a cup of tea and dunked his biscuit in it. And the taste set him thinking of when he was a kid. He wrote seven books about it, called *Looking for Time*, or *No Time to Lose*, or such. What stuck in my mind, though, was he did all his writing in bed. He just lay in bed and wrote. I could relate to that.

'A trigger for your memory can be anything,' Mr Robinson was saying, 'taste, touch, the smell of something familiar.'

'Like cat piss on the stairs in the flats,' said a joker at the back.

'That's it!' Mr R. jumped out from behind his desk and started down the room. They all shut up suddenly, as if they thought he was going to thump somebody. But, no, he was grinning all over his face and his eyes lit up behind his big glasses.

'That's very good, Trevor,' he shouted.

'It's not Trevor, it's Kevin, sir.'

'That's it!'

You couldn't get Mr R. down. He has a secret weapon. He never knows when anyone's taking the piss, cat or any other. He believes in people, like other blokes believe in UFOs, or kids believe in fairies. He always expects the best from you and he never notices when you let him down.

Tel had always come up to teachers' expectations. With me they cut their expectations down to size. I remember one report I took home. It said: 'He has an inquiring mind. It is a pity the inquiries often lead nowhere.' My mum was livid when she read that.

She was all for going down and tearing a strip off our form tutor. But Dad talked her out of it. He thought it was funny. He thinks a lot of things in life are funny.

My mum's small and wiry. Dad's big and bulky. I'm as tall as him and thin as her. Nothing ever bothers him. He's an electrician-plumber and all those stories about plumbers forgetting tools are true. He forgets to chase people for their bills as well, it embarrasses him. It doesn't Mum. One bloke owed Dad a packet and he wasn't about to pay. But she went round there with a blowlamp and the other gear and started to cut out all the hot-water pipes Dad had fitted. The bloke paid up.

My mates often grumble about their parents, but I quite like mine, though I keep quiet about that 'cause it's not cool. To hear my mates you'd think they all live in remand homes. Except Tel, he didn't mind saying his parents were right on. He was an only child and you got the idea they thought he was just this side of perfect. My parents didn't feel like that. They've been sort of relaxed about me.

I came late, a long way after the others. There's Sis – she's the oldest, with three of her own kids already. Her kids call me Uncle Mack (I'm John Macklin). Then comes my brother Callum, then ten years behind him, me. I was sitting on the stairs one day – I often do that, thinking. And I heard our Sis in the kitchen – ''Course, Johnny was your little mistake, wasn't he?' and Mum answered, as if she knew I was around, 'No, he was our little afterthought. Oh, our Johnny's all right, when he gets going.'

Sis laughed: 'That'll be the day.'

'Leave your little brother alone. He'll do something special one of these days.'

'If he gets a push.'

I never got pushed. Tel did, though. His dad expected a lot from him. He was always saying, 'My dad told me, I've got to . . .' My dad never told me I'd got to do anything. He always talks as though I understand already (he's often wrong). Mainly he tells stories that start, 'When I was your age . . .', his one trouble being he can never remember that he's told the same story twenty times before.

Like the one about when he was an apprentice and he was helping a craftsman set up some machine in a woollen mill. The electrician was up a ladder and must have put his screwdriver in the wrong place. There was a big blue flash and he was shot off on to the ground. He lay there, not moving. Dad didn't know what to do, so he put a jacket behind the bloke's head and opened his shirt collar. Next moment the sparks opened his eyes. 'Now, lad,' he said, 'what did I do wrong?'

Dad reckons you can always learn from your mistakes or other people's – in fact it's the only way you learn anything. What he didn't tell me was there's always the risk you'll learn too late.

Two

I started remembering for real a week into the holidays. I'd been out down town and was on my way home. But as I came into our street I stopped short.

There was a black limo outside our house, and it was familiar. I'd seen it before, some time ago, but where?

I went in through the back. We never use our front door ('Weddings and funerals only,' says Dad). Anyway, I was heading for the kitchen.

'What's for tea, Mum?'

Mum was sitting by the table reading. It was her speaking. She often does that, thinks it's funny.

'Stop messing about, Mum,' I said. 'What's for tea?'

'No tea tonight, Johnny.'

'You're putting me on.'

She shook her head, then nodded to the inner door. 'Your father wants you, in the front room.'

'But I'm starving.'

'Oh, don't be daft, lad, you'll get your tea after. Get a move on. They're waiting for you.'

They? That black car?

As I walked into the front room, Dad was facing

me. He gave me a wink, so quick I'd have missed it if I wasn't used to him. Then he said, 'John, this is Mr Holbrook.'

In the other corner, in an armchair, away from the light of the window, this bloke was sitting, black suit and dazzling white shirt, cuffs with gold cufflinks, like a life insurance man. His face was solemn and official, like someone from the council. There was a line between his eyes.

'Good evening,' he said, very formal. I was being sized up. Life insurance?

There was a silence you could cut with a knife. I sat down on the end of the sofa. Dad's eyebrows twitched and I shifted over to a dining-table chair. This was an interview – Head's office . . . Then I knew who it was. Of course I did, with that name.

'We haven't spoken before,' he said.

But we had. Somehow I knew that. He seemed taller then though, looking down on me. Now he was almost crouched in that chair.

There was another silence you could chew. Dad cleared his throat.

'Terrance's father wants to ask you –'

Mr Holbrook cut in. 'If you don't mind, Mr Macklin . . .'

Dad's eyebrows went up but he said nothing.

'Have you seen Terrance lately?'

Those dark, almost black eyes were weighing me up again. My mind wasn't on the question, at least not in the way he meant. This was stupid. I almost said, 'No, not for a week, he's on this world tour.'

Then I stopped in my own mind. If Tel was on a world tour, why wasn't his dad with him?

'Johnny, Mr Holbrook asked you . . .'

'Sorry, Dad. I haven't seen Tel . . .' I stopped at the look in those eyes, because I suddenly heard this little prissy voice: 'My name's Terrance, with an A and two Rs.' I started again. 'I haven't seen Terrance since a week ago, when he said he was going away.'

'Where?' Mr Holbrook leaned forward.

'He was going on . . .' I thought quickly – world tour sounded even more like a put-on now – '. . . on holiday.'

'What holiday?' He didn't believe a word I was saying.

Dad cleared his throat. 'I do think you ought to tell John that –'

'The fact is –' Mr H. took over as though Dad hadn't opened his mouth – 'Terrance has not been home for a day or two.' He seemed to be gritting his teeth. 'Sometimes boys stay with their friends.'

I shook my head so hard I felt it would fall off.

'I haven't seen Te – Terrance. I've no idea where he is – honest.' I could see Dad looking at me and cut it short. The longer you go on, the less people believe you.

'And your other friends?'

The question came out like a bark and I started to stammer.

Dad put his oar in. 'Perhaps, Mr Holbrook, you'd better ask Terrance's other friends for yourself. That is if you absolutely will not go to the police.'

I looked at Dad. It was funny to hear him putting the boot in.

'Terrance is *not* missing. Terrance would not do that kind of thing.' His mouth was a tight line.

'But he must have planned to go away?'

'Why?' The question was like a shot out of a gun.

'If he told John he was going on holiday.'

'Mr Macklin, Terrance has always been brought up to tell the absolute truth. We are a – very traditional family. But in recent times –' he looked slowly at me, then back at Dad – 'perhaps because of the company he's been keeping, Terrance has been a little less than frank with me.'

Now the eyes swung back to me again: 'Why are you smiling?'

'I'm not.'

Now Dad was looking at me. What I meant was that I might be smiling but I knew I shouldn't be. I didn't think it was funny. It was just ridiculous.

Tel wouldn't have smiled. His mind worked very quickly. He always did what was right – I mean what you're expected to do. But he was also something else. In my mind I could see, written on a wall, 'Tel is a roten liar'. Somebody couldn't spell, but they had our Tel sized up. You could not believe a word he said. When he said he was going on a world tour, I just knew it was rubbish. But he must have been going somewhere.

Thing was, where and why?

Three

When I got round to the caff that evening they were talking about – guess what?

'His dad came round to our place,' I started to say.

'Join the club – he's going round everybody,' said Rick, 'and you know what, when I told him Tel was on this world cruise, I don't think he believed me.'

''Course he didn't,' said Jamie, when the laughter died down.

'No, stupid. What I mean is he didn't believe that little Terrance told me he was going on a world cruise.'

'So, what did he believe?'

'I tell you what he didn't believe, he couldn't credit that his darling boy could tell porkies.'

'Not any more,' I put in, and told them what Tel's dad had said about him picking up bad habits from his friends. That silenced them.

Lumber spoke up. He hadn't said anything till now – he doesn't speak much, action's more his line, though he's not all that quick on that either. 'What I don't understand is –'

'We know what you don't understand – anything.'

Lumber ignored Rick. 'What I never understood

is how Tel gets away with it. I mean, if I came out with some of the rubbish he does, my mum would be on to me like a shot. But his dad thinks he's . . .'

'Little George Washington?'

'That's it.'

'Well, mate, telling lies is an art form. And our Tel boy is a master.'

'How d'you make that out?' I said. 'Everybody knows he's a ligger.'

'Right,' said Lumber. 'Hey, you remember somebody wrote on that wall? "Tel is a roten liar".'

'That's it – they couldn't spell,' Rick remembered.

'You're getting off the point,' I tried again. 'How does Tel get away with it?'

'Because we know he's a liar but they don't.'

'Why don't they?'

'Because we don't tell them. Listen, Mack, if you knew where Tel had gone, would you tell his dad?'

I didn't answer. Somebody laughed.

'The difference is, Tel's dad'd know Mack wasn't telling the truth.'

'Why?'

''Cause his ears light up when he fibs. Mack's a nice boy.'

'Belt up, Rick. Where do *you* think Tel is?'

'On a world cruise.'

'Seriously.'

'He might be sleeping rough,' suggested Jamie.

Rick laughed. 'Get a life. Whatever Tel is doing, he's doing all right. Did you ever know him do owt that wasn't good for Tel?'

'Don't know,' I went on. 'Maybe he had to get away. I mean, all those guys on the street, they're not there 'cause they like sleeping in cardboard.'

Jamie started to sing, or moan more like:

'He's got to get out,
To get out from under,
Out of that town . . .'

There was a general shout: 'Where d'you get that rubbish from?'

'It's a Mandate single, isn't it?'

'Bug off, mate.'

'So who wrote it?'

'No idea. Look, whose shout is it? I bought last night.'

'Don't look at me.'

They seemed to have forgotten Tel already. But I couldn't, and when I walked home the words of that song were still going round and round in my head: 'Got to get out, to get out from under'.

They went round and round because I couldn't remember any more. There were some other words dodging about, just out of hearing, inside my head. I had a feeling they mattered.

But I couldn't remember. The doors in that long corridor stayed shut.

Four

Next day I was at a loose end, what's new? I wandered round to Sis's place. I often do this and she doesn't mind – well, she doesn't seem to. As soon as I have my hand on the back door handle, I can hear the kettle going down on the cooker. Tea's ready just as I settle into the broken armchair in the corner and little Debbie or the twins crawl all over me. How Sis manages to do her paperwork in a kitchen that's so small you can cook, eat and do all the washing-up without moving from the same spot, I don't know. But she does.

Callum, my brother, and his wife, Phyllis, they have a kitchen like a spaceship. I've seen it but I've never been in it. I've never been invited and I wouldn't just wander in. I've never been told not to. I just wouldn't. Their place is different from Sis's. It's bigger altogether for a start and it's up the hill from town for another. Cal runs his own business, making commercials for television. Sis's husband, Wally, is an orderly at the hospital down town. I don't often see him. He works long shifts.

I don't often see Cal for that matter. I hardly ever go to his place, whereas I drop in on Sis when I feel like it. In our family nobody ever tells you you should or you shouldn't, you just know.

And that's another difference. Sis is often round, chatting with Mum. Cal and Phyllis hardly ever come, and as soon as they come, they're off again. I heard Dad say, 'It's like having a pair of whippets loose in the house.'

When I was little, I thought Cal was God. He could do anything, he knew everything. He'd help me with my maths.

'Look, our kid,' he'd say, 'it's easy.' But somewhen, maybe when he finished college, he just seemed to go off me. After he married it was like he was a total stranger.

Now that was weird. All those thoughts went through my head from the time I started to cross the road to the time I put my head in at the kitchen. I know I move slowly, but I'd no idea I could think so fast. In fact I wouldn't have started thinking about thinking, if it hadn't been for Mr Robinson. But once you start playing around in your own head, you can't stop.

Sis handed me a cup and the biscuit tin and scooped Debbie off my chest, all in one movement. Then she said, 'What d'you reckon's happened to your friend?'

My mouth fell open, then I realized that she and Mum always chat on the phone, after breakfast. No secrets in our family. That's never bothered me before, but now I started to wonder. Then I thought, no, that's stupid.

I said, 'You know, Sis, I don't really know anything about Tel.'

'But you've known him for years, haven't you?'

'Yeah, but . . .' I thought about our group at
school and now at college, people I saw every day.
How many did I really know, more than their names
and the way they carried on? Maybe half a dozen,
the ones I met in the caff. And what did I really
know about them?

Sis was looking at me, rubbing her cheek against
Debbie's.

'Haven't you ever been to his place?'

I shook my head, though I had the feeling that
wasn't true. I had been, but when?

'That's the funny thing, Sis. Tel was always on
about his dad and his mum, but I don't actually know
much about them.'

'How d'you mean, Johnny?'

She refilled my cup.

'Well, Sis, Tel was the biggest liar I ever met.'

'But you stayed friends?'

I stared at her. What had that got to do with it?

'If I found I couldn't trust someone, I'd have nowt
more to do with them.'

Sis was right. But it doesn't work like that. She
went on, 'Where would you look for someone if
you can't trust a word they say?'

I put my cup down. 'Who says I want to find out
where Tel is?'

Sis laughed. 'Oh, I thought that's what you'd come
round here to talk about.'

Had I? She picked up my cup.

'Right, Johnny. On your bike. I've got work to do before Wally comes in for his lunch.'

As I opened the back door, she added, 'His dad's creating all over the place. But what about his mum, eh?'

Five

'Tel's mum?'

Lumber's voice at the end of the phone went right up the scale as if he'd had an accident. Then he talked in his normal voice, more in sorrow than in anger. 'You woke me up to talk about Tel's mum?'

'Woke you up? It's eleven o'clock.'

'Too right it is.'

'You're still in bed?'

'We're on holiday, remember? Listen, Macker. You do this to me again and . . .'

'I'm in lumber.' I finished the sentence off for him. That reminded me of where big Gary got his nickname. It also reminded me of something else, but I couldn't remember what. Like you see someone out of the corner of your eye, and when you turn round they've gone and you're not sure if you saw them or not, except that you are – like sure.

'No, it's a serious question, Gary.'

Using his real name calmed him down and he said, 'Listen, Tel's mum, she works in that cake shop on the parade. You know, Irene's, it's called. She's blonde and – you know. You must have seen her.'

Yeah, I had. Suddenly I could see her face quite clearly. She had green eyes and she had a way of touching your fingers when she gave you change that made you heat up. Well, it embarrassed me anyway.

As I put the phone down I remembered something else. Tel reckoned he wouldn't go in the cake shop because his mum was always giving him extra cakes and Irene didn't like it. So he stayed away so his Mum didn't get into trouble.

One of his stories? It probably wasn't true, but I must have believed it at the time because – well, it wasn't important. And anyway it could have been true. That was the thing about Tel's little tales, and some of his big ones, they sounded true. They were like creative writing.

With all this going through my mind, I reached the parade. At least all this was running through my mind whether I liked it or not. That's another thing about your head. It doesn't do what it's told, it pleases itself what it thinks about, as though there's someone else in there. Then when *you* want it to work something out or remember something, there's, like, nobody at home.

The cake-shop windows were steamed up a bit. It's a sort of caff as well, with a couple of tables and chairs. Inside I could see this big busty red-haired woman in white overalls, that was Irene, and a girl from my year tied up in this overall thing two sizes too big for her. But there was no one who was like Tel's mum, or like the woman I thought was Tel's mum, which was just as well since I had no idea what I was going to say to her.

'Yes?'

I was standing by the counter. The girl from school was serving someone else. Irene was staring at me. She must have spoken a couple of times. I bought a Danish and was just about to go out when I thought, now don't be stupid, ask her. So I did, and got a real glare.

'She doesn't work here now. She went away.'

'Where to?' It sounded cheeky the way I said it, though I didn't mean to be.

'What d'you want to know for?'

'I've got a message for Tel, for her son.'

I could see the girl from school looking at me from further down the counter. I tried to keep my voice down. Irene gave me another withering glance. Then she reached up and took a postcard off a notice board behind her.

'She sent this after she went. Can't read the post-mark. It's supposed to be funny.'

I looked. The front of the postcard was dead black. In the middle was a light bulb and underneath it said, 'Illuminations in Scratby'.

Scratby?

She put the card back and started serving another customer. The girl from our school gave me a smile. But she soon wiped that off her face, because Irene told her to get on with her work.

I cleared off out of the shop, nearly forgetting my Danish. My mind felt like an evening in Scratby – with the light out.

Six

I finally asked Dad after breakfast next day. He stared at me for a while before he burst out laughing.

'Where did you hear about Scratby?'

Which was what I hoped he wouldn't ask me, but I guessed he would, so I had a sort of answer ready. 'It was on this postcard – somebody had.' I described the picture.

He nodded. 'Scratby's nowhere, Johnny.'

'That's a big help, Dad.'

'Thought you'd say that. No, lad, Scratby's always the other place, anywhere but your own town, the one down the road, the one across the river. Scrat's another name for Old Nick.' He looked towards the kitchen door and lowered his voice. 'It's also a nickname for blokes who are . . . like . . . you know.'

I nodded.

'Didn't this card have a postmark?'

'Couldn't make it out, Dad.'

'Typical. Sorry, Johnny boy, can't help you. Does it matter very much?'

'Nah. Thanks, Dad.'

What to do? I walked down to the caff. Did it matter? Why was I doing this, like poking around asking questions about Tel and his family? Did I think he'd gone off with his mum? If so, how come his dad reckoned he didn't know? In any case, did I really care where he'd gone? I wasn't sure, because I wasn't sure about Tel. He wasn't really a mate, was he?

You can know a bloke for a long time and he can get on your wick, but you can't get him out of your life. He's always there because he's always been there. When you think about it, I never liked Tel. There are blokes you like. You stop seeing them, but you know if you ran across them you could chat to them easily.

With Tel it was different. You didn't like him, but you had to take notice of him because of his stories. You could, in a way, depend on him for the unexpected.

That got me into the caff. Lumber was there, and Rick and Jamie and one or two more. I tried Scratby on them.

'What is it, Macker? Can you get treatment for it?'

I told them about the postcard.

'That's a joke?' asked Rick.

Lumber started to chuckle. 'That's not bad, illuminations,' he spluttered over his coffee.

The others looked at him pityingly.

'Hey, the light's gone on.'

They started tapping his head. He put up with it for a second or two, then he pushed Rick and Jamie off their chairs. Big Nick came out from behind his counter – he used to work down the pit – looking ugly.

'That'll do,' he said.

They picked up their chairs. I left them to it and walked out.

I trolled down to the canal bridge and walked along the towpath. Last year they'd cleared away the old ruined warehouses and cleaned up the rotten, sunken barges. Now it was all cabin cruisers and narrowboats with flowerpots and a clubhouse. I liked it better the old way.

One thing about our town, ten minutes' hard walk and you're in open country, meadows, woodland and further off the moors and hills. The sun was warming up and I slowed down.

There must be a reason why I wanted to know where Tel had got to. And the only reason I could think of was off the wall, actually. It was that I felt I knew where he'd gone, if I could find out what was behind those doors in the corridor. And that would answer the other question: why had he gone?

It must have to do with how things were in his family, or how things weren't in his family. He'd always given you the impression it was all marvellous, while other people ran their own family down or pretended to. But if things were so terrific, why did his father talk about 'I' and not 'we', and why had his mother gone off to Scratby – wherever that was?

Suddenly I felt this pain in my stomach. I was hungry. I'd walked for miles. I turned and limped back.

'Your dinner's in the oven. Your mother's out at work today,' called Dad from the front room, where he was watching an old Western with the sound off. He reckoned they were much better that way.

I got my dinner out, burned my fingers and swore. Dad's face appeared round the kitchen door.

'Never imagined you knew that word, Johnny, but we live and learn. You're old enough to use oven gloves, you know.'

'Thanks, Dad.'

He ignored my sarcasm.

'By the way, I met an old plumber this morning at the dump. He says, in the old days, when it was still an iron town, Scarsbridge was called . . .'

'Scratby,' I yelled.

'That's my boy.'

Seven

Nothing turns out the way you expect.

Like Scarsbridge. I'd never been there, but I knew what it was like. It's thirty miles from where we live. But you could see it, from the top of Haggerton. I mean you could see this dirty yellowish cloud on the skyline. And at night there'd be a reddish glow, like a sunset, only north not west. Dad said, 'Scarsbridge, a pillar of cloud by day and a pillar of fire by night.' I think he was quoting from the Bible. Funny how you half-know things you never learned.

Anyway, no more fire and no more cloud. They'd closed the ironworks down and sacked all the blokes. No idea where they went to. So Scarsbridge was depressed – officially. I wasn't looking forward to going there. I could picture it, rows of roofs in the rain like *Coronation Street*, shops boarded up, piles of rubble.

I didn't tell anyone I was going there, certainly not my parents. They only ask questions and find out things. I know that was what I intended to do, but that's different. I could have made up some story, but what? Off to Scarsbridge for a day out? Get a life.

I drew out fifteen quid from the post office. That left another fifteen, and that was another reason for not talking about it. I told Mum I 'might not' be in for dinner and she told me, 'Well, there might not be any left when you get home.' She was only joking, I think. But she looked at me, not any special way, just a bit longer than she usually does. I nearly broke down and confessed, but I managed to keep my mouth shut.

It was all different. The sun was shining, though nothing special in that, we'd had a heatwave since term end. The train to the junction was half empty, but when I changed for Scarsbridge and got into this two-compartment thing that smelt like an oil stove it was crowded, with kids and parents; there were even a couple of Yanks in white suits and half a dozen Japanese loaded with cameras. Where were they going? Was I on the wrong train? For a moment I panicked, then the driver said over the intercom, 'We are now approaching Scarsbridge.'

I looked out of the window. We were rolling down this long slope between green banks and hedges. Ahead there were lots of trees and white buildings, some tower blocks.

We drove under this huge signboard – 'Welcome to Scarsbridge' – and into this big open station, all glass and ironwork, with shop fronts and restaurants painted green. As the train stopped, the loudspeakers opened up: 'This way for the Heritage Trail.' The kids and their mums, the Americans and the Japanese nearly flattened me as they stormed out, heading for the coaches lined up at the exit. 'This way for your journey into the past.' I heard the coaches rev and the guides talking away. 'Scarsbridge was once the heart of a major industry.'

I looked round the almost empty forecourt. How did I begin my journey into the past, because that was what it was? I'd come this far and I didn't really know what to do next. How do you look for a woman you've hardly ever seen in a town you've never been to?

I looked round for a telephone. Then I stopped. Would she be in the book? When did she move? Tel had never said anything about his mum moving out, but then he wouldn't, and if he had done, it wouldn't have been true. There was a directory hanging on a metal rod. And it was in one piece, no bits ripped out, no stuff scrawled over the front. Scarsbridge *was* living in the past. I looked through for the Holbrooks. There were five.

A deep breath and I began dialling. One rang out and didn't answer, one was an answerphone with a man's voice: 'If you have a message for Percy Holbrook, please speak . . .' (that was a non-starter – if she'd moved in with somebody, the phone wouldn't be in her name, unless it was her brother). I put the receiver down. The third was an old girl: 'Is that you, our Ronnie? You'll have to speak up.'

I ran out of change and hung up, walked over to the restaurant and bought a coffee and doughnut. Half-way through it I realized there was a better way of looking for Tel's mum. She'd worked in a cake shop, why not look there? But how many of them were there in Scarsbridge? With all the tourists, there might be dozens, and then caffs, she might be work-ing in a caff. The only place she wouldn't be working at was the ironworks. Or she might be on the social. I was getting depressed. Still, I stopped at the cash desk and asked for Mrs Holbrook.

The cash lady looked blank. 'We've a Cartwright and an Armstrong and a Pirelli, but no Holbrooks, love.'

I wandered out. There was another place in the forecourt, a 'Tea-shoppe' – specially for heritage trai-lers, maybe. 'Cup of tea, please.' I couldn't face another doughnut, so I bought a sausage roll. It sank down on top of the doughnut and rested there.

'No Mrs Holbrook here.' The woman at the coun-ter gave me a quick look, then asked, 'Is that her married name?' I hadn't thought of that. 'What's she look like?' Have you ever tried describing someone, I mean someone you know, never mind someone you only half remember seeing.

'She's like blonde and she smiles.'

'Oh, ah?'

I found a cake shop in Station Road, then another on the High Street. This time I settled for coffee. My stomach was getting clogged.

'What does she look like?'

'She's like blonde and – she's got green eyes.'

Did I make that up? It came out just like that. The woman gave me a funny look. And as she was saying, 'No, we've got no green-eyed blondes here, lad,' I realized something else and burst out, 'Do you, like, have a loo here?'

She shook her head. 'Up the road, behind the post office.'

I just made it. The relief was incredible and I was standing there, looking at the white tiles with the water running down them, when I remembered something. I walked outside and sat on a bench opposite the town hall. People were milling around me, but I wasn't seeing any of them. I was walking down this corridor in my mind. But whatever it was I'd remembered about green eyes, it had gone again. All the doors stayed closed.

Slowly I got up. Down the High Street to Market Street. Another coffee, another tea, a packet of biscuits to soak it up. Now I was counting my cash as well as crossing my legs, and I was getting nowhere, apart from back to the Gents behind the post office.

I'd almost given up. I'd worked round in a circle and could see this sign, 'To the Station', at the end of the street. Gritting my teeth, I pushed open the door of this little cake shop, deciding this was going to be my lot. And there behind the counter was this woman, I don't know how old, but blonde, smart-looking and smiling. And suddenly I remembered about the green eyes.

I'd been in the cake shop back home. There was a bit of a queue and I was behind this big bloke in overalls, like a gas fitter or something. As she – Tel's mum, I mean – gave him his change, he leaned forward.

'Be round at one o'clock.'

He wasn't asking, he was telling. She had a funny

look in her eyes. I think she saw me looking at her. She stared at me, like a dare, and I looked away. Afterwards I must have forgotten all about it. Now I thought of something else, and that's the funny thing. You see something you don't understand, but you remember it as if you had done – well, as if you knew there was something odd about it but you couldn't think what. He didn't mean he'd be round to the shop at one o'clock. He meant somewhere else and that could only be her place. And that bloke wasn't Tel's dad, at least it wasn't the bloke in the black suit who came round to our place the other night. Who was it? Did it matter?

What did matter was – if that was Tel's mother, then this was Tel's mother looking across the counter at me now.

Eight

'Yes, love?'

She stood there in her white overall with this funny white hat on the side of her head and smiling in a way that made my face start to go warm. I don't know how long I stood there. I felt totally stupid. I wanted to go, but that would have made me look even more stupid. My mouth opened and words came out. They weren't what I meant to say, but they did the trick.

'I've come about Tel.'

'You what?'

Her face went hard. Those smiling green eyes turned cold. They stared through me.

'I mean . . .' I was stammering now, couldn't get the words out properly but couldn't stop them. 'Like . . . Terrance . . .' When I used his proper name, I could hear this posh little voice, in the junior school: 'My name's Terrance, with an A and two Rs.'

She moved so quickly I jumped. She was out from behind the counter and standing in front of me.

'How did you find me? Who sent you?'

It was like she was going to hit me. She only came up to my shoulder.

I swallowed. 'Nobody sent me.' My voice ran up

– I could hear it echoing in my head. 'I'm just looking for Tel. He's – missing.'

That stopped her. She didn't know that, I could tell. Now she looked away. Her face was older all of a sudden. Someone called from the back of the shop.

'What is it, Sharon?'

'Nothing, just a lad asking the way.'

She put her hand on my arm and lowered her voice: 'It's my lunch-hour in ten minutes. Meet me in the station, by the ticket office. OK?' She gave me a push towards the door. Her eyes were friendly again, almost smiling.

I paced up and down outside the ticket office, excited. I'd worked it out. I'd found her – on my own. But how was I going to play this? I'd thought maybe Tel was staying with her, but now I wasn't sure. And if he was, would she let me know? What was going on?

'Are you right, love?'

I turned round. She was standing there and at first I didn't recognize her. She'd taken off her overall and was wearing a short red dress. And she'd made her face up.

'Let's go and sit in the park. It's not far.'

As we walked she chatted. 'Have you been here before? It's not a bad place. I didn't like it at first.' No, I thought, sending postcards with jokes about Scratby. 'But it's very clean, not like it used to be. There's a lot going on.'

In the park she put her arm through mine and steered me over to a caff with tables outside. 'You wait there,' she said, went inside and came out with a tray of tea and sandwiches.

'I often come here for my lunch. Sit and watch the world go by. You often meet – quite interesting people.'

She looked at me over her teacup. 'You're very shy, aren't you? What's your name?'

'John – John Macklin. I'm a friend of Terrance's.'

'Oh, you can call him Tel if you like. It was his father who always insisted on Terrance. He was – is – rather strait-laced. I'm not.'

I cleared my throat. 'Tel's missing from home. His father came round to our place the other night, asking where he was. So I thought maybe he was . . .'

'With me, eh? Well, he's not. I'm all on my own.'

My head started to spin. 'Then you don't know where Tel is either?'

'I don't.'

Her tone was flat and final, as if she was talking about a stranger. And this was Tel's mother.

'You know, John, he tried to run away from home before.'

I must have looked baffled.

'I thought you were supposed to be his pal. Didn't you know that?'

'No, honest. I never heard.'

She made a face. 'Not surprising, really. He'd tell his mates he'd been ill or on holiday. He'd come up with some yarn.'

I nodded. 'He did tell some stories.'

She started to laugh. 'John, love, he was the biggest little liar I ever met, was Terrance. You could not believe a single word he said. I gave up trying to sort out what was what with him long ago.'

'So you've absolutely no idea where he might be?'

'No, and I don't . . .' She stopped and looked closely at me. 'You see, he wasn't my son. He was nearly fourteen when I married his father. And even then he was into fairy stories. I did my best. I did my best with him. I, I don't know why I'm talking like this to you when we've only just met. But you've got that kind of face, John . . . nice and open.'

She reached across the table and rubbed the back of my hand. 'I bet the girls are after you.' Then she laughed again. 'Oh, I'm making you blush. I like it when a feller does that. It means they're very nice – deep down. You know, it's funny, John, we've only just met for the first time, but I feel I've known you for years.'

Not the first time, I thought – I was behind that bloke in the queue in the cake shop back home.

She jumped up. 'Have you had enough like? Let's go for a walk.'

Her arm was through mine and as we strolled out of the park gates she gave mine a little squeeze.

'I'm sorry I can't help you. I'd love to. I was a bit sharp with you when you came in the shop. But I didn't know who'd sent you and what you were after.'

We were walking away from the town centre. I looked around. She read my thoughts.

'Don't worry, John –' another squeeze – 'I'll see you to the station afterwards.'

We turned down a side road. She was chatting away as if we were the same age. How old was she? I was trying to work it out. It didn't seem to make any difference to her.

'There's no hurry. I get a good lunch-hour. I often pop back to my place just to relax. It's just down here.'

She looked sideways and up at me and squeezed my arm again. All of a sudden my brain seized up. I pulled my arm away. Now I was talking fast.

'Just remembered. I'm catching an early train back. They'll be expecting me for supper.'

I heard her say, sharply, 'Oh, run along home then.'

And I did.

Nine

I caught the train by the skin of my teeth and sat there squashed between the kids, all sticky with candyfloss, and the Japanese tourists. But I didn't look at anybody or anything. My head was in a complete mess.

What did you run away for? one part of my mind asked the other. She wouldn't have eaten you. I could hear Rick and Jamie across the caff table: 'Macker, you are a complete waste of space. You get a come-on like that and you take off.'

Their voices sounded so real in my imagination, I had to tell myself – they won't know. Nobody knows, but her and you. Then the other half of my mind answered: That's enough, isn't it?

You might have found out some more about Tel, like what his home life was really like. No, I wouldn't. She wasn't going to say any more. And anyway, could I have believed it? How did I know Tel's mother – well, his stepmother – wasn't as big a liar as he was? She had a whole life her husband knew nothing about – or did he?

What I did know was that Tel's picture of a happy family was rubbish. Had I ever believed that? I suppose I had, 'cause, why not? Why shouldn't other people's families be like ours, no big deal, just getting on? Maybe – the thought just crossed my mind as the train rattled along towards the junction – my other mates were just saying their parents were the pits because everybody moans about their mum and dad. They wouldn't admit they liked them, even if they did. With Tel, it was the other way round.

Wherever Tel had gone, it wasn't with his mother. As far as she was concerned, he was history, along with his father. She must have given them a hard time. Was that why Tel cleared off? 'Cause he couldn't stand rows? Do you leave home because your parents fight? I wouldn't know.

There was a long wait changing trains and this time I had to stand – it was rush hour. My thoughts went back to where I was before. If the way his mum carried on made Tel clear out, why did he wait till she'd gone before he vanished? The more I went over it, the less clear it all seemed. And I was still no nearer to working out where he had gone.

The train jerked to a stop. I was home. As I got out among this stream of commuters and struggled up the slope from the station, someone was shouting. 'Help the homeless.'

Over by the fence a big red-faced bloke with a massive beard was selling the *Big Issue*. I caught sight of this picture on the front of the paper, taken with a flash at night. A lad my age, curly hair, pale face, was sitting on a broken wall. It could have been Tel. Was he out there somewhere, living rough?

I couldn't believe it, but the thought made me shiver.

That night, for once, I lay awake. I was thinking about my Scarsbridge trip. I went over all I'd said to Tel's mum, and what I ought to have said, what I might have done. In the end I fell asleep out of sheer frustration. But not before I had this idea.

I was up early – well, early enough to have breakfast with Mum and Dad. I had to put up with remarks about not being able to sleep. I just let them pass over me. It wasn't so easy dealing with questions about what sort of day I'd had. Nothing crude or direct like that. My family never goes full-frontal. They just worm things out of you.

I told them a story about my holiday assignment, gathering material, ideas about the past. I had to go careful not to overdo it. Too much information makes them as suspicious as too little. As I talked my eyes went first to Mum, then to Dad. In the back of my mind I was thinking about Tel, how he looked straight at you with those wide-open blue eyes and talked the most amazing bullshit you ever heard. It was an art form and I was no good at it.

I don't think Mum and Dad believed me altogether, but they weren't going to make an issue of it. They let it pass. They had other things on their minds.

So had I. I went back to the station where the commuters were streaming back down the slope they climbed last night. From inside the station the loudspeaker was playing music – marching music. It made my feet move more quickly. Before I knew where I was going, I was almost inside the forecourt. If I hadn't got hold of myself, I'd have been on the train heading for work – if I had a job.

I stopped in my tracks and looked round. Our friend selling the *Big Issue* was over by the fence. I swam across the stream towards him.

'Thank you, sir. Cheers. Good luck,' he was bawling as every now and then someone gave him money. I kept out of the way by the fence, but he'd seen me and when the rush had died down he turned.

'What do you want, son?'

'Can I have one of your papers?'

'You can indeed.'

I gave him a pound and said, 'Can I ask you something?'

He laughed, a big raucous laugh, which made people further down the slope turn round.

'For a quid I'll tell you what day it is.'

'It's about a friend of mine.'

He looked closely at me, then spoke more quietly. 'Let's go up the brew to the transport caff and you can buy me a cuppa. They don't like me in the station restaurong, they think I frighten the horses.'

He folded the rest of his papers under his arm and led the way up the slope. The transport caff, which is a long, low shed sort of place, was crowded. The bearded bloke seemed to know somebody at every table. We found a place in the corner and I brought over the teas, hot and brown as gravy, in big, thick mugs.

'Right, son, who are you and what do you want? You don't look like a nark, too young and innocent, but you never know. Just lately I've become a bit suspicious of my fellow human beings.'

I told him my name.

'Macklin?' he said. 'Is your old man a plumber?'

I nodded.

'That's it. Thought the name was familiar. I used to be in that line myself, till – never mind about that. Now you tell me, John – my name's Porter by the way, at least that's what suits me.'

I fished in my pocket and pulled out Tel's passport photo. 'He's missing from home and I wondered if . . .'

'What's his name?'

'Terrance Holbrook.'

'Not the undertaker?'

Undertaker? That rang a bell. But Porter went on, 'How long's little Tel been gone?'

'About a week.'

'Kipping with friends?'

'None of them know owt.'

'Parents split up?'

'Yes, but he's not with either.'

'You have been poking around, haven't you, Johnny boy?' He shook his head. 'Wherever Tel boy is, it's not the usual places, the hostel, behind the library, the arches. If he's on the town, I'd have seen him.' Porter handed back the photo. 'If he really has

39

cleared off, I'd say he might be in London, on the streets.'

'You what?'

Porter waved his hand at me. 'No need to shout. Just a thought. You'd be amazed at the sort of kids who end up like that, some out of choice, most 'cause there's nowhere to go.'

'Tel wouldn't do that . . .'

'How d'you know?'

How did I know? I mean, what did I know for sure about Tel? The truth might be weirder than the lies.

'Tel's a bit of a romancer.'

Porter's laugh was like a bark. 'Your pal tells pork-ies, eh? Join the club, John. Let me tell you, if our Tel isn't a liar already, he's going to learn very quickly. When you're on the street, the truth has no meaning. No, that's not what I mean. There is one big truth – no one gives a damn what happens to you. You don't tell the truth because it doesn't help. Why did you leave your last job? Have you got any form? Have you got any savings? Tell the truth and do they say, 'good lad'? No, they say, on your bike or we'll cut your Giro, or we'll have to tell someone about you.' He waved his arm in a broad sweep. 'When you're on the town, everything normal is just virtual reality – a steady job, family, a decent meal, warmth, a good night's sleep. And for every one who helps you, a hundred walk past or look right through you. You don't exist, you're transparent, you're only there because you don't like work. Truth, Johnny?

Think yourself lucky if you know what it is. In this game you work out a good story and you try and remember what it was every time.'

'Can I get you another cup, Porter?' I asked.

'No, thanks, son. Got places to go. I'd love a nine-to-five job, Johnny, I could take it easy then.' He stood up. 'If I see him, I'll tell him you're looking for him. But I'd be very surprised if you ever see him again.'

Ten

I was getting nowhere, inside my head or outside it.
Wandering round town, drinking Coke at Nick's,
sitting at home staring out of the window, walking
along the canal, walking and thinking in circles.

Where had Tel gone? I'd tried his mother. She
didn't know and couldn't care less, though I still
found that hard to credit. I'd tried Porter. He hadn't
narrowed the field, he'd thrown it wide open. Tel,
on the streets in London? Porter had said, 'if you
ever see him again'. That made me feel sick.

Why was I bothering when I didn't really like Tel?
You have to trust somebody, a bit at least, if you're
going to like them. So why was I spending so much
time, moling around trying to work out what had
happened to him?

Why did I feel responsible for him? There was a
reason for that too, if I could work it out, if I could
open one of those doors in that dark passage.

One morning I was on the High Street, aimlessly
looking in shop windows. I stopped by the off-
licence and looked at the posters. They were throw-
ing the stuff at you, buy eight, get four free, get
drunk, make us happy. Then down at the foot of
the window display a word in an advert caught my

eye, about sherry: 'Amontillado'. A bell rang in my head, faint and distant. I tried to think back. Why was that word special? But I couldn't get hold of it. The memory wriggled away out of sight. But it was still there and in the middle of the night I suddenly found myself thinking 'Amontillado'.

Next day I felt I must do something positive. The Numero Uno question was what and where, yeah and how? I'd got a cash-flow problem. I was down to my last quid, unless I raided the post office again, in which case I'd soon have nothing left at all.

Borrow from home? No way. I didn't want to tell them what I was up to, did I? Because they would tell me not to – that's the main reason for not telling anyone what you're doing, isn't it? Apart from which, when I got home they were in the middle of one of those quiet tussles they have now and then. They never shout or throw things. They're very patient with each other, but the air crackles with static.

It was about bills, I could tell that, even though they stopped when I walked in, but whether it was bills they had to pay or Dad's bills his customers weren't paying, I couldn't tell, and in any case – same difference, no use talking money to them.

So I ended up going to our Sis, strolling round at about four in the afternoon when I guessed she'd have the kettle on. She knew a bit of what I was doing anyway and I could talk to her about Tel and maybe I could raise the matter of a small loan.

Big mistake. No, three big mistakes.

43

She did not want to discuss my Quest for Tel at all. She did not rate it as a subject for conversation. In fact she said, 'Don't you think you ought to leave this off, Johnny? It's for his parents or the police. You go on poking around and you may get more than you bargained for.'

I tried to tell her over a cup of tea about my trip to Scarsbridge. But she stared at me. 'You did what? You traipsed round the town hunting his mother? You want your head seeing to. Why do you think she left this place?'

'But you said yourself, his mother might –'

'I thought he might be with her. I didn't mean you should go snooping on her.'

I suppose, then, I should have kept my mouth shut about bankrolling more fact-finding after that, but I didn't. Sis is normally so helpful and patient, it just seemed natural. Mistake No. 2. She bit my head off.

'Do you think I've won the lottery or something, Johnny? Did you say ten quid? I haven't got ten pence to spare right now.'

I said sorry. She made a face at me as though she were sorry as well. 'Would five help?'

I shook my head. 'No, honest, Sis, it doesn't matter. I was being stupid.' I said, 'See ya', and went.

She shook her head at me as I left. Little Debbie called out, 'Bye, Uncle Mack', and I realized I hadn't even talked to her. I felt very low.

But my biggest mistake, No. 3, had already happened when I arrived at Sis's. As I came into the kitchen the door to their front room was open but someone was closing the door quietly and clearing their throat very softly as they did so. I said, 'Oh, sorry, have you got company?'

Sis shook her head. 'No, Johnny.' But her cheeks were pink and I could tell from the sound that there was a bloke in the front room. As I moved off down the road, I tried to put it out of my mind. My life was getting complicated enough. I did not want to know any more about Sis's private life, did I? Once you start poking round trying to solve mysteries, you find out things you do not want to know.

To get these thoughts out of my head, I started to think about Amontillado. It wasn't just the one word. It was several words including that one. But what?

Mulling over this got me back to our street. But I hadn't finished with surprises for the day. There was still one with my number on it.

There was a police car on the other side of the road. It was outside our house.

Eleven

As I came in through the back and the kitchen, I could hear voices from the front room: Mum's, Dad's, then a bloke's voice, slow and official. It's possible in our house to go from the kitchen, along a little passage past the front room and up the stairs, if you go quietly, which I did.

In fact, I had my foot on the first step when Mum raised her voice. 'Well, our John's just come in, he's on his way upstairs now, so you can ask him yourself.' I took my foot off the stairs.

There were two of them in the front room, a tall thin bloke with sergeant's stripes and a policewoman, good-looking with a nice smile. Well, she was smiling at me. He wasn't. His eyes were narrowing as if he were trying to remember something.

'John, lad,' said Dad, pointing to the dining-room chair in the corner – all the comfy chairs were taken – 'Sergeant Taylor and WPC Chesters want a word.'

'Right,' said the sergeant. 'Your father put my central heating in,' he went on, as if that made everything all right.

WPC Chesters smiled at me again, which did help. I heard somewhere they bring a WPC along with them if they're not going to beat you up, but these days you never know.

'I expect you've guessed –' Sergeant Taylor was still trying to put me at ease – 'we're here about Terrance Holbrook.'

Before I could think, I said, 'But his dad said he wasn't for involving the police.'

'Ah.' Sergeant Taylor was looking at me more closely, as if he suddenly made up his mind I was smarter than he thought. 'Well, John, there's no harm in telling you that Terrance's father has become increasingly concerned. Technically he's a bit old, your pal, for us to be looking for him, but there are exceptions to the rule. Mr Holbrook's worried Terrance may do something silly.' He paused, weighing me up again. 'A – certain sum of money has gone missing from their home.' He paused, then there it came: 'Is there anything you'd like to tell us?'

I took a deep breath. 'Well, I have sort of been looking around to see if anybody knows where Tel – Terrance is.'

'And you've no idea.'

'No.' I raised my voice, which is never a good idea. The louder you speak, the less they believe you.

'Ah, his mother seems to think you might know.'

So, she'd been on to the Law already. I was way off beam about her.

'I can't make out why she thinks that. In fact, I went to see her to –'

'You went to see her?' Mum and Dad sang out in chorus.

Sergeant Taylor made a little move with his finger and they stopped.

'I thought she could tell me where he was,' I finished.

'Ah, but she couldn't make out how you found her. She thought Terrance must have told you something.'

'Well, he didn't.'

'What did he tell you?' Sergeant Taylor was on to me like a ferret.

'I mean he didn't 'cause he couldn't, 'cause I haven't seen him, 'cause I can't find him.'

That shut them up for a second or two, then WPC Chesters asked, 'Just as a matter of interest, how did you find out where she was?'

I told them. Why not? Dad burst out laughing. Mum said, 'Shh!'

'Cake shop?'

Even Sergeant Taylor smiled, a thin smile. 'Well, John, I suggest you leave the investigations in our hands.'

I didn't answer. What could I say that would be the truth yet still leave me a free hand?

They got up to go. Sergeant Taylor handed me a card.

'If you feel, ever, that there's something you might tell us, here's my number. OK?'

As they reached the door, Dad was there already, holding it open. I think he wanted to see the back of them as much as I did. But Sergeant Taylor turned in the doorway.

'Haven't I seen you before somewhere, John?'

'No,' I said automatically. But I wasn't sure. I mean, how can you swear you've never seen someone? You can swear you have, but never, ever? The outside door closed and Dad came back into the room, shaking his head.

'You know, Johnny, you reminded me of something from when you were quite small.'

'Oh, no, Dad,' I protested, thinking he was going to tell one of his stories, like the one about me putting my fingers in the power point and my nose lighting up.

'What do you mean "no", Johnny? What I was going to say was, when you were younger you always wanted to be a detective. You sent off for a special offer – magnifying glass, pad for doing fingerprints . . .'

'Right,' said Mum, 'your fingerprints were all over the woodwork for weeks afterwards.'

'Give over, will you?' I was beginning to get irritated.

'All right,' said Mum. 'Listen, we're taking you off this case. If anyone can find your pal, the police can.' She shook her head. 'You know, I never knew you thought all that much of this lad. I thought he wasn't all that trustworthy.'

You have no idea, Mum.

'Yes.' Dad picked the ball up. 'Find something else to do for the rest of the break, eh?'

I said something then so crafty it almost stopped me in my tracks. 'I'll do some more work on this holiday assignment, like writing down things you remember from earlier in your life.'

They looked relieved. I felt guilty. It was the first really non-spontaneous porkie I'd ever told them.

The amazing thing about it was that it was true. What wasn't amazing, but very, very disturbing, was that when I was on my way upstairs, later on, I remembered where Sergeant Taylor had seen me before.

Twelve

When I was sure the Law had gone and my parents were settled for the evening with a survival programme about monkeys with coloured bums, I went out to Nick's. Rick and Jamie were there already. They were always there already. They spent the day in the caff. But how could they afford it?

Stupid question. As I pushed open the door, Rick called out, 'Three teas, Macker's paying.' Nick looked at me. He knows them as well as I do. I shrugged, said, 'OK', then to the pair of them, 'That's the last freebie from this end – get it?'

'Ooh,' they said. 'Is the dosh running out?'

Rick nudged Jamie. 'He spent it all on a wild trip to Scratby.'

Jamie nudged Rick. 'Was it exciting, Macker?'

I ignored the questions. There was no way I was going to tell them I'd actually gone there, nor about finding Tel's mum, much less about the police coming round to our house. There's only one way to stop people asking stupid questions. Ask some yourself. I picked up the teas from the counter and as I did Rick shouted, 'Make that four, will you?'

Lumber was in the doorway looking as though he'd just got out of bed. I was glad he'd turned up, because I was sure he'd remember what I was going to ask about. When we were all sitting down I began.

'You remember that time the Law came round here?'

'Oh ah,' said Jamie. 'Nick banned us all for three months afterwards.'

'Keep your voice down.' I didn't want to remind Nick about it.

Rick stared at me. 'What are you so narky about all of a sudden?'

'I'm asking the questions,' I told him, narrowing my eyes like Sergeant Taylor.

'They won't remember it,' Lumber was talking now, 'because those two were nowhere to be seen.'

'What does that mean?' demanded Jamie.

'It means,' Lumber went on, face red with concentration, 'that when the trouble started, you and Rick did a disappearing act, leaving Macker and me here with four blokes from the High.'

Lumber spoke so firmly that neither Rick nor Jamie tried to argue. But Rick said, 'Wasn't our fight anyway. That little creep Tel started it. I remember that, though I haven't a clue what it was about.'

Lumber spoke bitterly. 'Tel was showing off.'

'So what's new?'

'He was bragging about his karate, doing a Black Belt course he reckoned. Told us how his instructor beat up fifteen blokes in the boozer one night. He was demonstrating when he knocked this bloke's cup off the table and that started it.'

I could remember it now, the way all of a sudden Lumber and I were on our own against four of them, chairs flying, Nick storming out from behind the counter and then the police turning up. After that the drama turned into farce, because Tel told the police sergeant (which must have been Taylor) this incredible lie about stopping these other blokes being rude to a poor old lady. Nick persuaded the Law to go away again, but he told us and the blokes from the High we could stay away until he was ready to have us in his caff again.

Now I remembered Sergeant Taylor's face, listening to Tel. He couldn't make up his mind whether this was totally untrue or not, but for the moment he was fascinated.

I suppose I forgot all this detail because at the time being barred from Nick's seemed more earth-shaking. And there was something else I'd forgotten.

'Oh, yeah.' Lumber was still bitter. 'Karate Black Belt – and what was worse, he was going to sign on for the Paras.'

There was a laugh round the table. Tel in a red beret. That was good. But why was Lumber so narked? It began to come out.

'There was no way he'd have got in.'

'Too young?'

Lumber brushed this aside.

'You can fiddle your age. They're not that bothered if you've got what it takes.'

'Like what?' I asked. An idea was forming in my mind – off the wall maybe, but an idea. I tried to speak casually because I didn't want Lumber to get suspicious and stop talking, which he would do very easily.

'Like height, weight, fitness, motivation.'

We all listened.

'I sent off for the info . . .'

We stared at each other.

Rick said, 'You were thinking of joining the Paras?'

'Why not?' Lumber caught the tone of the question and was indignant.

'You mean,' Jamie joined in, 'you reckon you had what it takes?'

Lumber glared: 'As a matter of fact, I do.'

Rick and Jamie exploded in laughter. I kept my face straight.

'Knock it off,' I told them, then asked Lumber quietly, 'Did you – like – follow it up?'

Lumber's face suddenly looked miserable.

'Well, didn't you?' needled Rick.

Lumber wouldn't answer.

'Come on, tell us,' coaxed Jamie.

'Leave it,' Lumber growled, sticking his face into his cup.

'I know,' crowed Rick. 'His mum wouldn't let him.'

Lumber jumped up, his chair falling. Nick's head shot out from behind the urn. But Lumber had rushed out of the caff, slamming the door so the windows rattled.

I grabbed up the chair. 'You prat,' I snarled at

Rick. 'What did you do that for, just when . . .' I stopped. I'd nearly said too much.

'Just when what?'

'Just when nothing,' I threw at him as I ran out of the caff.

I caught up with Lumber at the end of the High Street. It took a while to calm him down. But when I'd convinced him I wasn't laughing at him, he slowed down.

I got him to talk at last and it was true his mother was dead against him joining the Paras. 'She'd be on her own, see.' But he was still dead keen.

When I thought he'd cooled down enough, I began to explain my idea to him. Well, the idea really began to take shape there and then.

He listened to me, frowning. Then he said, 'What's in it for you? You don't want to join the army.'

I told him.

'You're crazy.'

'I know. But are you on?'

'OK.' He put out his hand and we shook on it.

Thirteen

What I planned to do was daft, though I did crazier things later on. Yet at the time my idea seemed brilliantly simple. I wanted to talk to some of the blokes at the Para depot in Walkington, which is a good forty miles away from our town. On a long chance I wanted to ask them about Tel. Lumber was keen too, he just wanted to have a look inside the camp, meet some of the Paras.

The big problem was the folks at home. My mum and dad would not have liked it; Lumber's mum would have gone spare. Fortunately I had the answer and it was so simple. In a week's time, Mandate were doing a gig on an old airfield outside Walkington. It was so ingenious. Lumber's mum would be happy because he was going with me. My people would agree because I was going with him. There were a few loose ends.

'How are you getting back?' asked Mum.

I was ready. 'There's a train from the junction at one a.m.'

'And if you miss that?' she demanded.

'If he misses that,' put in Dad, 'he can give us a ring and I'll pick him up. In fact, you can give us a ring when you leave Walkington, just to be sure.'

He's crafty, in his way, but what he said suited me.

'Can you afford the tickets?'

'Lumber – I mean, Gary's seeing to that.' I blushed when I said that, but internally if you know what I mean.

'And the fare?'

I took a chance. 'Wouldn't mind a loan,' I said quickly, so quickly Mum looked at me, suspiciously. I was learning, but I still did not have the artist's touch.

Still, the show was on the road. Half-way through that Saturday evening, Lumber and I found ourselves walking round the streets of Walkington. They were pretty empty. Faintly in the distance we could hear them warming up for the Mandate gig. The old folks at home were in for a treat. In fact, there aren't many streets in Walkington, it's a bit of a dump, and I suppose that's why they put the army barracks here, so the blokes'll stay in and polish their buttons or whatever.

There were two caffs and they were half empty.

'Nobody in uniform,' I announced.

Lumber looked at me. 'What rock have you been on? They don't go out in uniform. They wear civvies, like human beings.'

'How're we going to pick them out?' I asked.

He looked sadly at me. 'By their haircuts. They look as if they've been in the nick. When you go in, they shave it all off for you.'

'And you still want to join?'

He shrugged. 'It'll grow again.' He looked at me. 'We'll have to try the pubs. You got any spare cash?'

'Eh?'

'Well, mate, if we're going to find owt out, we're going to have to buy a drink or two.'

I did have a bit in my pockets. I'd cleaned my account out. But I hadn't bargained on treating the Parachute Regiment, though how I thought I was going to pursue my inquiries without doing that I can't think. My plan, in fact, had holes in it. Just how many I found out later.

The main street must have had about fifty pubs – big ones all lit up like the *Titanic* and mostly empty. There must have been some serious drinking in the old days. But in the first one there were only the barman and an old couple with a dog, and he wasn't drinking. We stepped out again smartly.

The second was just the same. But when we looked in the third, I knew we were in luck. Near the door was a longish table with six young blokes – well, when I say young, they were older than us. They all seemed to have blond or ginger hair and blue eyes and they were all big and tough-looking and making a lot of noise in an amiable sort of way. At first they ignored us as we took our shandies to the next table and started to sip and ponder the next move.

Should I go up to them and say, 'Hey, fellas, the Milky Bars are on me'? Or should I walk round with Tel's picture and say, 'Have you seen this guy?' Or, 'My friend here is thinking of joining the army. Do you have any career advice to offer?'

I needn't have bothered. The next stage of the plan just fell into place. We were sitting there pretending to talk to each other – I think Lumber was even more embarrassed than I was – when I realized that one of the soldiers, the biggest in fact, was giving us the once-over. He was a good-looking bloke with a strong jaw and sunburnt face. His teeth showed white and he had smile lines round his eyes. He looked straight at me, but in a friendly way.

Then he spoke. 'Not at the gig then?'

We shook our heads.

'Not interested?'

'Not much.'

He turned to his mates. 'Well, fellas, a sign of intelligence in this godforsaken hole, two blokes who don't want to listen to that crap.'

'We don't belong here,' I said quickly.

'Even better,' he answered. What did that mean? Before I worked it out, he shoved his next-door neighbour. 'Make a bit of room, Scouser.'

'What for?'

'So these gentlemen can join us.'

I was amazed to see how the others shifted their chairs at his word. He nodded to us. 'Join us?'

It was an order. We stood up.

'And another thing – if you're going to sit at our table, you drink what we're drinking – Old Tom.'

Lumber was suddenly wary. 'I don't know.'

'Aw, come on!' The whole table was shouting to us now.

'Yeah, come on,' I urged Lumber quietly. 'This is your chance, you know.'

We shifted our chairs over. They called to the barman and we had pints in front of us as soon as we'd sat down again.

'My name's Charles, believe it or not,' said the leader, 'but they call me Chuck. This is Darren, Tod, Cliff, Scouser, Taff.' He went round the table.

'I'm John, this is Gary.'

Chuck said, 'We're in the Regiment.'

'We guessed,' I said, taking a long pull at my pint just to show I was at ease.

'What's that mean?' said Scouser, a broad bloke with arms as hairy as a gorilla's. ''Cause we look like a bunch of thugs?'

'No,' I protested.

'There you are,' shouted Chuck. 'Disappointed, Scouser?'

'Up yours, Chuck,' came the polite response.

Chuck turned to me. 'The truth is, John, most people think we're a bunch of animals, though they don't mind us doing their dirty work.'

I saw my chance. 'Well, my mate Gary and I don't think so. We wanted to have a chat with you.' I was further down the glass and Old Tom was beginning to do the talking for me. I could see out of the corner of my eye that Lumber wasn't drinking as quickly, but by then it didn't bother me.

'Oh, you did. Why?' Chuck's voice had changed – he was almost eager.

The others were quiet, wary.

I pressed on. 'Two reasons. One, I'm looking for a mate of mine who talked about joining the Paras.'

'What's his name? What's he look like? If he's come here we'd know him all right.' Several spoke at once.

I dug out Tel's picture, a bit crumpled now, and handed it over. Chuck gave a quick smile and passed it on. The others weren't so polite.

'Who's pulling what?' said Taff.

Chuck half raised his hand and suddenly another bloke spoke up. 'Hang about. I'm sure I saw this one somewhere in the depot. Looks a smart little sod. Wouldn't trust him.'

Chuck got hold of the picture and handed it back. 'Tell you what. How about we ask back at camp? He might have come and gone, like a lot of blokes do. What was the other reason, John?'

'My mate,' I began. I felt Lumber pushing his foot against mine, signalling like, but I ignored it. 'Gary's interested in joining.'

'Now you're talking,' said Scouser. 'We might make something out of Gary.'

A laugh started, but Chuck silenced it and turned to Lumber. 'A lot of kids think they'd like to be in the Paras, 'cause they've seen a few films. But when they get closer, they don't like it and then it's a bit late. They don't like it.'

'You mean it doesn't like them,' said Taff.

Cliff put on a Lance-Corporal Jones voice: 'They don't like it up 'em.'

'Shut up,' commanded Chuck. He turned to me.

'We do get a lot of recruits who join without knowing what they're in for.'

I nodded as if I knew already.

Chuck gave a quick look round the table, so quick I almost didn't see it at the time, though I remembered it after.

'If you two are really interested, why not come back to the depot with us? I'll square it with the guardroom. You can have a look round, bite to eat in the canteen. Then if your friend's still interested, he'll know what he's taking on. What d'you say? We've got the wagon down the road. It's only two miles. We'll drop you back at the station after.'

Lumber hesitated, but I urged him on. 'This is your chance Gary. And there may be someone up there who's seen Tel.'

'That's my boy,' crowed Chuck. 'Come on, fellas. Drink up and we're away.'

Fourteen

A grey-green truck with an open back was parked down the road and we all piled in. There was a lot of laughing, pushing and shoving, and effing and blinding. Every few words there was some crude comment. Even in my somewhat woozy state I remember thinking, 'It doesn't mean anything to them – it's just a way of talking.'

Deeper down in my mind I was realizing they were excited, not with booze, but like kids up to something. I realized something else. They were practically kids, only a year or so older than Lumber and me – just fitter and tougher.

I was getting excited too. This bloke had said he'd seen Tel. Maybe I was going to pick up the trail.

The truck swung left round a corner, right round another and roared into open country. The others fell about in the rear of the truck, pushing one another to and fro and shouting, 'Cheer up, Gary, it may never happen.' But Lumber was saying nothing, just staring in front of him. If I didn't know him, I'd have said he was scared.

'You know what's wrong with our Gary?'
'No, what's wrong with our Gary?'

'He's not had enough to drink, that's what's wrong with our Gary.'

'We'll see about that – after.'

'Right, after.'

The words came out in a singsong and the voices got louder till Chuck turned round in the front of the truck and said crisply, 'Belt up in the back, will you? We're nearly home.' Then he said, quietly, to me, 'When we drive in, you two sit well back, will you? We have to check in at the guardroom, right? And you are unofficial – get it?'

'OK,' I said carelessly, as though I did this every Saturday night.

The truck turned off the road, men shouted; there was the slam of boots on concrete.

A big bloke, in uniform, red beret set square on his forehead, white armband on his sleeve, was glaring into the back of the truck.

'Who've we got here then?'

Chuck appeared at his side. 'Couple of blokes from B Company, we picked 'em up in town, out of their skulls. We're putting 'em to bed.'

'You are one of nature's gentlemen, Cuffley,'said the guard and waved his arm.

Chuck's face vanished, the truck door slammed and we rolled into the camp. Light was fading, but I could see rows of brick buildings, green plots fenced off with whitewashed posts and ropes – even the ropes were whitewashed.

The truck stopped dead. Someone thumped on the side: 'Let's be having you. Out, out, out.'

We burst out of the truck so quickly I sprawled on the ground. Someone hauled me up. My arm almost came away from my shoulder.

'Hey,' I protested.

But I was being urged on, so fast my feet barely touched the ground. There was a moment's confusion, everyone crowding into a narrow space, and then we were through into a larger room. Lights came on overhead. I could see beds, tall lockers, big posters of topless women.

'Here we are then,' said Chuck quietly. 'John and Gary are our guests for the evening.'

We were standing in the middle of a black, polished space and the others were round us in a circle. I somehow knew this wasn't right, but . . .

'We promised to show them what it's like to be in the Paras. Something only the chosen few ever find out. Even John and Gary only qualify after they've passed the test.'

Now there was silence. The air was tense. I could feel the blokes in the circle brace themselves. But my muscles were going slack, my head empty, my stomach cold.

'John, Gary, are you ready?'

Lumber and I looked at each other. Lumber said, 'What's going on?'

'I'll tell you in a minute,' Chuck said with a wide smile. 'First though, get your kit off, both of you.'

Fifteen

'Wha-at?'

I could feel my jaw drop. I must have looked stupid.

Chuck repeated, patiently, 'Get – your – kit – off, John. You can't take part in the entry test with your kit on, like civvies, can he, boys?'

'No, Chuck, he can't,' they chorused, and the circle moved closer.

Lumber suddenly moved. Yelling with fury, he lunged for the door.

Lumber's a big lad. But Scouser stopped him in his tracks and casually tossed him back across the circle. Cliff caught him and almost gently threw him back. Scouser turned him and bowled him to another part of the ring. I could see his eyes roll in his head.

Lumber fell against me and we both fell to the floor. Six faces looked down on us, all smiling.

Chuck spoke. 'Come on, Gary. Come on, John. The sooner we start, the sooner we finish. Aaah!'

Lumber's foot whirling round caught him on the ankle.

'Gary, you should not have done that, should he, boys?'

'No, he should not.'

'Right, what is the penalty for non-compliance?'

They all seemed to know. The circle closed on us and we were lifted up like dolls and raised in the air. My mind had shrunk to a small point in my head.

The lights went off. There was a scuffle of boots on the floor. The ring was breaking up. Suddenly let go, we sprawled on the ground. From somewhere I could hear a great crashing noise and a voice bawling.

'Open up. Open up!'

'The back,' I heard someone whisper.

Another tremendous crash. The outer door flew open. The lights went on. Inside the room was one of the biggest blokes I've ever seen, in uniform with three stripes on his sleeve. Just behind him, I saw the man with the armband from the camp gate.

As we struggled to our feet, I was amazed to see Chuck and the others in two rows, rigidly at attention as the huge sergeant walked slowly towards us, his feet pounding on the polished floor.

'Corporal, these men to the guardroom, at the double.'

As Lumber and I gawped, they jog-trotted in single file past the door, which was leaning off its hinges.

Chuck hung back though. He spoke. 'Sergeant!'

'Yes, Cuffley?'

'This was just a lark. Gary and John will tell you. They asked if they could see over the camp – get the feel of it.'

There was a silence. How cool Chuck is, I thought.

'If you ask them, I'm sure they'll tell you it's OK.

I don't think the company will get any comeback over this. In any case, we don't need to go public . . .'

The sergeant seemed to swell. Then he spoke quietly. 'Just one mistake, Cuffley. We are not talking little tricks. I've had my eye on you for some time. I'm not going to charge you with stupid, dangerous horseplay. You are going to be charged with breach of security. Cuffley, this time you are for the high jump.'

As Chuck marched through the broken doorway, the sergeant suddenly turned to us.

'I'm Sergeant Harris. Are you lads OK?'

We nodded.

'Will you come over to the Mess with me? We'll get you some supper and perhaps have a chat about – this.'

Ten minutes later we were working our way through the biggest pork chop with chips and peas that I've ever seen, while Sergeant Harris, drinking beer from a big tankard, watched us.

'Right, John, Gary. Tell me how it all happened.'

I told him the lot. I even showed him Tel's picture.

He looked at me. 'You believed them when they said this lad had been in the depot?'

I shrugged. He said nothing but I could see he thought I was one short of a full set.

He went on, 'It goes without saying, you get a full apology, here and now, for what you've had to put up with. But I hope you won't mind my saying, you were a bit unwise. There is no way, John, that this mate of yours would have been accepted by this or any other unit. Does he usually come up with stories like that?'

We said nothing.

'And there is no way, normally, that other ranks are allowed to bring civilians on to the base to look round.'

I could see Lumber looking miserable. I changed the subject.

'How did you, like, find out, Sergeant?'

He nodded. 'The guard commander saw you in the truck. Cuffley said you were from B Company. Now Gary here, he fitted, but I'm afraid, John, you did not fit. They thought it over and gave me a call.'

While the sergeant talked, I was narked to see that Lumber had a little smile on his face. He was chuffed because he looked the part.

'Now, the question is, do you wish to make a formal complaint? That is your right.'

I looked at Lumber and spoke quickly. 'Not me, Sergeant. I feel stupid about the whole business.' I pushed on. 'I talked Gary into coming along.'

Sergeant Harris nodded. 'What about you, Gary?'

Lumber surprised me. 'I'll think it over, Sergeant.'

There was a nod. To my amazement, the sergeant seemed to approve of Lumber's attitude. In fact, I was getting more miffed by the minute with the way he seemed to think Gary was OK while I was a bit of a waste of space. But then, I wasn't queuing up for a place in the Paras, was I? And I guessed that Lumber had cooled off a bit after this evening.

'Right, lads. Let's get you home.'

'There's a train at the junction at eleven-thirty,' I put in, wanting to sound clued up.

'No, door to door for you two tonight.' He lowered his voice. 'In a way you've done me a favour. We've been trying to crack down on this sort of thing – with new recruits, as it happens. The trouble is, blokes join the Regiment with expectations of excitement. If there's no action, they start doing stupid things. People on civvy street don't understand. They want professionals to do – well, the dirty work. But they expect nice boys at the same time. It doesn't mix. My job is keeping a balance. Otherwise, blokes like Gary get put off and blokes like you, John, think we're a bunch of thugs.' He stood up. 'Sermon over. Let's go. Sorry I can't help you find your pal, John. I think he's living on another planet.'

I got home around midnight, persuading Sergeant Harris to drop me at the end of the road. I walked in to find Mum and Dad watching the late news.

Mum jumped up. 'There you are, Johnny. I was worried sick.'

My mouth fell open. What did they know? I tried to sound nonchalant. ''Course I'm all right. Why not?'

She nodded towards the box. 'The riot at the concert, Johnny. We saw pictures. The platform was wrecked, the police were there. Dozens arrested. We thought you'd have phoned us.'

I was thinking on my feet. 'Oh, we left Walkington before that got going. Anyone who wasn't a mug could have seen that coming.'

Tel couldn't have done better.

'Did you enjoy your evening then?'

'Oh, it was interesting enough.'

Sixteen

I woke with a thick head, throbbing like a two-stroke, and lay there wondering if it was morning, afternoon or evening. It made no difference, 'cause I was nailed to the bed. The house was dead quiet, the authorities had left the building. I could lie here all day until the sky outside the window went dark. I didn't even have to eat. I didn't want to eat. But my mind was going round in circles. Why? Why didn't it play dead like the rest of me?

Slowly I worked it out and, as I did, I realized I had to get up. There was something I had to do. But what? There was only one way to find out. I started to go over yesterday: the pub, the truck, the barrack room, the humiliation, the sergeants' mess, the big supper, then the drive home and the story I told Mum and Dad.

That was it. I grabbed the thought as it wriggled away into the undergrowth inside my head. The cover story. What had Lumber told his mum? Had he told her anything yet? I had to get hold of him, agree stories like we used to in the corridor outside the Head's office.

My watch said nine-thirty. Was that morning or evening? If it was evening it was too late. I sank back. But if it was morning I could still ring Lumber.

Then came the really tough question. Would he talk to me? Last night, after the business in the barrack room, he'd hardly spoken, and when Sergeant Harris drove away from our street with Lumber in the back, he hadn't even said, 'See ya.' I couldn't blame him. Last night was all my fault really. He'd wanted to find out what it was like and now he knew. What made it worse was that it was really all because of Tel and his lies, lies, lies. Right now Lumber must be sticking pins in a doll with my name on it.

But I had to talk to him. If word should get back to the Macklin home of what really happened yesterday, I would be, in Sergeant Harris's words, 'for the high jump'.

When I can't solve a problem, my habit is to take cover. So I lay back and closed my eyes. I began to drift away.

The phone rang. It's in the hall. The sound travelled up two flights of stairs, round a corner, through my bedroom door and down my ear. I rolled out of bed, feeling sure it was some customer desperately wanting Dad to come and bail them out.

Crawling downstairs, I caught it just before it stopped.

'Mack?'

'Ye-es.'

'It's Gary.'

'I know. What d'you want?'

It shows how scrambled my brain was. It was me

who wanted to talk to him. But he wasn't bothered at all.

'Mack, I owe you.'

Now when someone says that, you've either got a favour coming your way or something you are not going to like. I decided it was the second and tried to distract him.

'Listen, Gary, what did you tell your mother last night?' and before he could say a word, I gave him my cover story. I was only half-way through when he started laughing.

'You are a prat, Mack. You're worse than Tel.'

'What's that supposed to mean?'

'I mean you're a rotten liar. You're no good at it.'

'Thank you.' Somehow I sensed that he was bursting to tell me something and, what's more, he wasn't itching to break bits off me either.

'So what did you tell her?'

'What d'you think? I told her where we'd been and what happened.'

'You did what?' I squealed. 'You need brain surgery. Correction, brain surgery's a waste of time on you. Where do you think that leaves me?'

Lumber suddenly sounded incredibly pompous. 'Look, what lies you tell your parents are your problem. But you can relax. My mum is not going to blow the whistle on you and neither am I.'

I became sarcastic. 'So, she's happy with the truth?'

'The truth's best in the long run, Mack.'

'You what?'

'Especially from the horse's mouth.'

'What horse?'

'Sergeant Harris, no less.'

'Sergeant Harris. Now you are off the wall, Gary.'

'No way. Look, when we dropped you off, I got my first real chance to have a word with him.'

'Your first chance?'

'Yeah. You were too slewed to stop yakking all evening.'

'You liar.'

'Takes one to know one. Anyway, to cut a long story short –' oh boy, was he pompous! – 'Sergeant Harris came in with me to talk to my mum. He was very persuasive, very impressive.' He lowered his voice. 'I reckon she fancies him.'

'So what did he talk to your mum about, his next night off?'

'That as well. No, the Army, stupid, the Paras. He answered her questions and – you know what? – next month we are going on a visit to the depot.'

'You *and* your mum?'

'Of course. She rather likes him and I get the spin-off. Love me, love my regiment.'

'So?'

'So, if all goes well, I get to sign on when I'm seventeen and a half.'

'Sign on? But you're nearly seventeen and a half now.'

'You are beginning to sound intelligent, Mack. Look, are you all right, Mack? You've gone all quiet.'

'Gary, I am sitting down, recovering from the

shock. You got just what you wanted out of last night.'

'Like I told you, honesty is the best policy.'

I blew a raspberry down the phone.

'So I owe you, Mack. I thought you had landed me in the doo doo, but you did not. I ought to be totally off you, because lately you have become impossible. But I am actually grateful to you. You see, I would not have been crazy, stupid enough to have gone there on my own, I wouldn't have . . .'

'Been beaten up by a bunch of teenage psychopaths.'

'Just horseplay.'

'You're talking like them already, Gary.'

'If it hadn't have been for you, Mack, and your lies, I would not have met Sergeant Harris. In fact, both my mum and I owe you one.'

'Stop it, Gary. This is stupid. I get you to come with me as a cover for hunting Tel. All I get from the evening is a pork chop. But you get your chosen career. Gary, you owe me more than one.'

'Like I said, Mack, I owe you . . .' Then he stopped, as though his brain had gone into overdrive. 'I owe you one, but that does not include anything to do with little Terrance Holbrook. Get it?'

'I see, not a very big favour then.'

'Listen . . .' Lumber spoke slowly. 'I do not think it is a favour to encourage someone to do something stupid.'

'What's stupid about looking for a pal?'

Lumber sounded disgusted. 'He is not your pal, is

Nineteen

As I climbed the stairs at the side of the health shop next day, I was excited and scared inside. Glenda as I'd met her in the pub was different from the fantasy picture I'd had, third-hand, via Tel. She was real, she was normal, she was as friendly as Sis. And I knew that his story was a pack of lies, didn't I? This was the thing that kept me on his trail though – there was some truth in it. She did exist. She did take him to her studio and I was going there now. Maybe, though, in that inside part of my head, I was wanting his crazy tales to be true.

At the head of the stairs was a door painted red and yellow in stripes and whorls. I knocked.

'Come in.'

Inside was a big room with windows along one side. It was a total mess, worse than my place at home, things piled on cupboard tops and tables, stacked against walls or just dumped on the floor. There were only two clear spaces. The middle, where she had her easel, and a big old leather armchair over by one wall. She was behind the easel doing something with brushes. But she stuck her head out and gave me a big smile.

'I knew you'd come. You're the reliable sort.'

'Me?' No one, but no one, had ever said that in all my life.

'Sit down and look out of the window please. We'll do half an hour, break for coffee, then half an hour more. That's as much as most people can take, OK?'

'Yeah,' I said, uncertainly. Sitting still was no problem, with all my experience, but where would we go from there? Still, worry about that later. I sat down and now I could see her properly. Her face was paler – maybe she'd been made up last night. But she still looked good.

'Not allowed to look at the artist. Pick a point out of the window and keep your eyes on that. Like Haggerton Top.'

I looked out of the window. There was a view across the roofs and out towards the moors. They were all lit up in the sun.

'Comfy?'

I wriggled about. 'Yeah.'

She suddenly came towards the chair, bent over me and took my face in both hands. For a second I panicked inside, but all she did was tilt my head a little on one side.

'Mind holding it like that?'

'I'll try.'

'You must do more than try, John. This is for real. This is work and I want my five quid's worth.'

So I fixed my eyes on Haggerton Top and after a while I began to relax, my thoughts wandered. I wasn't thinking about Tel, though, but about Glenda, comparing her with girls at school, some of whom were OK, but most of whom were hopeless. Well, she was older. How much? Maybe ten years or more, but I had this feeling that when she was seventeen she wasn't hopeless. I felt easier with her 'cause she was older. That takes care of a lot. I'm used to every-body round me being years older. You don't have to work on relating to them. I just felt comfortable . . . This was the life.

'OK, so let's talk about your friend. What can I tell you?'

I don't want to talk about Tel, I thought lazily. But I couldn't say that.

She went on, 'I didn't meet him in the Green Dragon, John, that's just fantasy. I saw him one day, outside the cake shop on the Parade. He was standing there looking in. His face was reflected in the window. It was lovely, like one of those cherubs in the Italian paintings – you know, little boys with curls and bows and arrows.' Her voice suddenly became professional. 'Keep still and do not look at me . . . No, I did not paint him in the nude. I didn't want to. It was that face, very good-looking, gorgeous eyelashes, as long as a girl's, and the look in the eyes, knowing, but underneath that something else . . .' She stopped and scrubbed at the sheet on the easel. 'Sod it. I'm looking at you and drawing him.'

'What else?' I asked.

'It was as if he was scared. No, not exactly scared. Haunted, John. You don't expect a teenager to look haunted, do you?'

I shrugged. How are teenagers supposed to look – madly, deliriously happy?

'I was saying –' she was busy at the easel again – 'I spoke to him, got him to come here. He came round about half a dozen times, sometimes for a sitting, sometimes just to talk.' She hesitated a moment. 'He brought me flowers, and chocolates. I think he had a crush on me and in the end he took a bit of shaking off. I had to be quite firm. I did not want him in my private life.'

While she talked, my mind was going round and round. Tel thinking about somebody else. Tel having a crush on someone. I could not believe it. It was like Tel speaking the truth. I suddenly felt stupid. I mean, well, jealous.

I tried to fix on something else, because these thoughts were making me uncomfortable, when suddenly she put her charcoal down and said, 'Coffee.' She went to a corner where there was a small sink and a kettle plugged into the wall. 'No you don't.' Out of the corner of her eye she had seen me move. 'You can't look at it until I tell you. Sorry, but that's an order.' She brought across mugs of coffee and pulled up a stool near my chair.

'When you gave him the push, what happened?' I asked awkwardly.

'John, I do not give people the push. I just asked him to be a bit sensible. I do not like it when blokes get boring. Friendship's a great thing. You can't get enough of it. But as for the other, well, that's something else.' She cut off that line of conversation, just when I was getting really interested, and said, 'John, I've been thinking. You said your name's Macklin, right?'

'Yeah, why?'

'Are you related by any chance to Callum Macklin, head of Media Mark?'

For a second I was dumbstruck, then, 'Cal's my brother.'

Her face went just a shade pink. 'Your brother, what a fantastic coincidence.'

'You know him?'

'We were at college together and . . . well, never mind about that. But later on we went different ways.'

'How d'you mean?'

'Well, he went into graphics, then advertising, started his own business – though you know all this, don't you? Now he's a millionaire, not that that's any big deal these days, there's a hundred thousand of them around. But there he is, head of a firm and I'm scratching around.'

I wanted to say, My brother's no big deal, but something stopped me. I was learning, these days, to keep my mouth shut, now and then.

'If you're wondering why I mention Cal, it has to do with your friend.'

I wished she wouldn't keep calling him my friend.

'The last time I saw Tel, he told me he wanted to get away from home, maybe find a job. I thought of Media Mark. It's full of kids with smart ideas. So I suggested he went there to ask for a job. Since then, I haven't seen him. Whether he actually went to your brother or not, I don't know. I'm afraid I just put him out of my mind until you picked me up in the Green Dragon.' She took my mug. 'Back to work.'

I looked out of the window. She worked at the easel and the sun shone into the room, picking up the fine dust in the air. I could feel my body going slack. I wasn't thinking about anything, certainly not Tel.

'OK, that's it for today.' She was shaking me gently. 'You fell asleep. Models do drop off now and then. Don't worry. We're doing fine.'

I blinked and struggled up from the chair, my head still muzzy.

'Can you – would you like to come for another session?'

'Like tomorrow?' I said quickly.

'Uh huh. Other things tomorrow. How about Friday?'

'OK.'

She handed me a five-pound note and pulled open the door to the stairs. I stood in the doorway, trying to think of something else to say. She smiled and shook her head, then reached out and patted my face lightly with her hand.

'See ya, John. Good luck.'

The door closed behind me.

Twenty

Brother Cal's company, Media Mark, was in a country house, ten miles out of town, well away from the railway, one bus a week, that sort of place. There was nothing for it but on your bike.

It was a brilliant day, again, and hot, of course. So by the time I was pedalling up this long winding drive I was streaming. My shirt was several shades darker and my jeans were pinching my sensitive parts. I must have looked a wreck when I finally stood in front of this enormous reception desk with this blonde, all knees and eyebrows, looking me up and down. I cleared my throat.

'I'm here to see my brother,' I began.

The eyebrows went up, the knees retracted. She became familiar. 'Well, I expect you'll want the warehouse, love. Outside, turn right and round the back. OK?'

'No, Mr Macklin.'

I thought the eyebrows would take off. She looked at me a second or two, then lifted the phone. Her voice lowered but I heard her say something like, 'Reckons he's the MD's brother . . .'

There was a pause. Her voice got lower. In the background I could hear more voices, a woman's then a man's. I heard her whisper, 'Yes, that sort of sounds like him.' Then she gave me a big smile and said, 'Would you kindly take a seat. Someone will be down for you in a minute.'

I sank into this armchair and picked up a mag from a glass-topped table. *Country Life*. I'd never read that before.

And I didn't read it now, because the lift door across the room slid open and out bounded brother Cal, tall, lean and ginger, beaming at me over those rimless half-glasses.

'Johnny! Great! Just in time for coffee.'

I was dragged out of the chair and hurled into the lift and we were throbbing up through the floors. Out into a long passage with framed posters on the wall, pots with feathery plants and then through a massive oak, brass-fitted door and into an office with a window so big I felt like a goldfish. There was another blonde, but taller and with no knees – skirt down to her ankles.

'Julia, this is brother John. Coffee and Danish, I think, big one for John, small one for me.'

I was swallowed up in another huge armchair and my mouth was full of apricot, icing and pastry. If I'd wanted to speak right then, I couldn't have. But, in any case, Bro was doing the talking.

'How's everyone at home, still the same, eh?'

Had he been in China? But then we didn't see him more than two times a year. He bounded up from behind his desk and sat on the front of it, swinging his legs. I remembered what Dad said about Cal and Phyllis — 'like having a pair of whippets loose in the house'.

Thinking of this would have made me smile if I could have got my teeth loose from this square yard of Danish.

'Mum still collecting Dad's bad debts?'

I nodded.

He ran on. 'Everybody does it — I mean doesn't do it — pay bills. They get passed on down the line until someone has to pay.'

How would you know, Bro? I wondered.

'Take the last gas bill. Sent three weeks before it's due. Please pay promptly, allow fourteen days for the cheque to reach us. Then the crafty so-and-sos say, "Please do not post-date cheques." So they get, say, one million dim customers to pay up ten days before they need and think of the cash flow that generates, eh? But get them to pay you ten days in advance or even ten days in arrears? I should coco.'

I felt I ought to say something. I took a swig of coffee and washed the sticky mess in my mouth down my gullet. But Cal hadn't finished. 'And Sis and Walter?'

'They're OK,' I burst out. I suddenly remembered the last time I'd seen her, just a week ago, though it seemed ages now. That bloke in the front room, her closing the door and seeing me off.

Cal rattled on: 'I admire our Sis. She works like a Trojan. She's got a first-class degree and she spends her time helping people who, between you and me, don't deserve it, and then there's Wally, slaving in that hospital that was built in the Dark Ages and smells like it. I don't know how they can do it.'

He jumped off the front of the desk and marched behind it, sat down and faced me, as if I'd interrupted him. 'Someone in this misguided family has to make some money, John.' He brushed his hand across his face. 'Look, Johnny, I have offered to help, not once but several times.'

This I didn't know.

'They don't say, "No thank you," Johnny, they just change the subject. They don't like the way I make my money and I don't suppose you do either, our kid.'

'I haven't said a word, Bro,' I protested.

He glared at me. 'I know what you're thinking. In my business, people's silences are as important as their words.' Then he smiled, like rueful. 'If I were on just ten K a year, they'd take a loan or whatever from me like a shot.'

He was silent. I took another bite of Danish and drank more coffee. I did not know what to say. I'd almost forgotten why I was here. But he solved that problem.

'Sorry, Johnny. That was a rant. You didn't come all the way out here to listen to me whingeing, did you?'

I struggled up out of my chair and placed Tel's grubby little picture on Cal's desk.

'I was told my mate Tel had come to see you. Is that right?' I hurried on before he could start. 'He's missing from home. I just wondered if you'd talked to him, if he'd given you any clue, like where he was heading.'

Cal stared at me. 'Why the Sherlock Holmes bit, Johnny?' Then he laughed. 'Yeah . . . I remember when you were ten, you had this fingerprint outfit, and a false moustache too.'

I blinked. Cal remembering anything about me.

'Aren't the police looking for him?'

'Yeah and not finding him.'

'Yeah.' He studied the picture. 'Is he really as old as you, Johnny? He looked about fourteen, except round the eyes, where he looked about forty. He came in and asked for a job. Said he was interested in ideas.'

'You turned him down?'

'Right. I thought he was out of this world, a fantasist. Wouldn't believe a word he said.'

'I don't know, Cal, I'd've thought that would be ideal in this job.'

He frowned, then smiled. 'All right, our kid, point taken. This business does deal in fantasies, but customers' fantasies. We have to see the world as it is. We sell real things. We can't say, "This car does 100 m.p.h. in fifteen seconds" when it won't hit forty even. But we are selling into people's dreams. You take that ad, "This car is not for the small-minded." The visuals suggest that anyone who buys it will be unique, unlike all their neighbours. But if that were truly true, how many actual cars would they sell? It's the way the punter feels when they get out their chequebook, that's what counts.'

There was a flaw in the argument, but I couldn't put my finger on it. Maybe Bro was telling himself, not me.

'But you didn't give Tel a job?'

'No. He had a quick, inventive mind, just what we look for, but . . .'

'But what?'

'Two things. He was desperate to get money. Someone in that state might stick their hand in the till. For another, I did not want a kid on the edge of a psychological black hole in the office.' He paused, as if he'd said too much. 'Sorry, Johnny. Can't tell you any more than that. How long has he been missing?'

'Just over a fortnight.'

'Hang about. He came here when he was on the run then. So how do you know he'd seen me?'

I told him, reluctantly.

'Hey, so you know Glenda? Well, I'll be . . . Is she doing well?'

I nodded. He hummed to himself.

'We were at college together. Don't suppose she'd wipe her paintbrushes on me today. She's another one thinks money's the root of all evil.'

I began to feel uneasy. I did not want to discuss Glenda with Bro. I couldn't find out any more about Tel. So I climbed out of the chair. He was on his feet, round the desk and grabbing my hand before my jeans parted from the leather.

'Well, our kid, all I can say is good luck. I think it's great what you're doing, though I'll be honest with you, I think you should watch it. My guess is that he is trouble, big trouble.'

We were at the door when he said quietly, 'Do you need any cash, Johnny?'

I shook my head. 'Thanks a lot, Bro. It's OK. I've got this – part-time job.' I didn't say what.

He dropped my hand. 'You're as bad as the rest of them. Well, see ya, our kid.'

Twenty-one

I'd come to the end of the trail with Tel. I had no more leads, no ideas. He'd vanished as if a UFO had landed and picked him up. And in my mind all the doors in that long corridor stayed closed. There was one that had the word 'Amontillado' on it, but even that wouldn't open.

The difference now was that it didn't seem to bother me in the way it had done. Maybe I had other things on my mind. Two mornings that week I climbed the stairs at the side of the health shop to Glenda's studio. I sat in the old chair looking out over the moors. Each day the sky was clear and the sun shone on the wall with the dust falling through the rays. Sometimes I'd buy cakes to eat with the coffee.

'You're a gent, you know that, Mack?'

Glenda had started using my nickname, which chuffed me no end. She grinned when she said it, but that didn't bother me. There's a difference between smiling and smiling at. She was working with paints now, but she still wouldn't let me look at the portrait. 'When it's finished,' she said.

We chatted about all sorts of things. I told her about going to see Bro, though I didn't tell her what he'd said about her: 'Don't suppose she'd wipe her paintbrushes on me today.'

She talked about art college, I talked about school. We discussed films, music, anything. Conversation was dead easy for me, for once. Though there was a lot of silence. And I worked out how to keep my head still with my eyes looking out of the window at the view, while every now and then my eyeballs swivelled round so I could look at her. I liked the way she screwed up her face and swore to herself, then scrubbed something out. The trick was to swivel them back whenever she looked across at me.

One day she caught me and said, 'The artist looks at the model, not the other way round.' But she smiled all the same.

I began to hope that this could go on right through the holidays. I was getting paid too, though I'd have done it for nothing.

But one day Glenda said, 'I'll take a break from you, Mack.'

'You what?'

'What I mean is, don't come till I tell ya.'

'Ah, why?'

'Working on something else.'

'Does that mean you've finished it?'

'Nah. Just a bit tired of it.'

Tired?

'I'll put it on one side for a bit.'

'Just like that?'

'Always doing it. Sometimes I put paintings on one side and forget about 'em for months.' She saw my face and laughed. 'Oh, Mack love, I was kidding, sort of. Look, let's make it Tuesday, OK?'

For the next few days I mooched round town. Lumber was nowhere. The phone didn't answer. He must be on the assault course or practising parachute jumps off a wall somewhere. Now and then I saw Rick and Jamie in the caff. But we didn't talk about Tel. We'd run out of memories of him. In fact, we didn't talk about much at all. I began to find their conversation a turn-off, actually. It was dead boring and I wondered why I'd bothered in the past.

Tuesday took its time coming. The weekend dragged. I even wandered round to the market and strolled idly past the health-food shop. But I could see nothing through the studio windows, just the shape of the easels. One evening I looked in the Green Dragon but no Glenda.

Tuesday came. I climbed the stairs, gave a quick double knock on the red-yellow door and marched in. Then stopped short.

There was Tel facing me across the room, head on one side, that little smile on his lips as though he'd just got away with another story. At the same time the eyes were staring, not light blue, but dark and hollow.

I blinked once, twice. Then I saw he wasn't standing in the room, he was up against a black wall in a narrow street. It was an almost life-sized picture of him.

'What d'you reckon, Mack?'

Glenda was standing behind the easel, with just a small, anxious look on her face.

'It's fantastic, Glenda,' I said. 'But, I mean, where did you do it?'

'Why, here, in the studio, Mack. Where d'you think?'

'But that street, the walls – it's great.'

'Oh, those – from my notebook. I can't ever do a portrait or a study without wanting to tell a story.'

'But where did you get the idea, like?'

'Listen,' she said, and turning to the worktop, where she kept the kettle, she switched on an old cassette recorder. A woman was singing, well howling a bit, I thought, with guitar in the background. At first I couldn't make out the words, but slowly they became clearer. I recognized them.

> A street with no name
> A park with no trees
> A house with no windows
> A kid with no future.
>
> So can you wonder?
> He's got to get out
> To get out from under
> Out of that house
> Out of that street
> And out, out of that town.

'Hey, what's that?' I asked Glenda. 'Who's singing?'

'It's called "Got to Get Out". Almost took off – a few years ago.'

'Yeah.' Almost is worse than never.

'I rather liked it. It says something. I was playing it the other day, for no particular reason, when I suddenly felt – that's how I'll finish Tel's picture.'

I nodded. It was good. But it was depressing!

Glenda seemed to read my thoughts. 'It's bleak all right. But maybe there's the answer. Tel's got out, gone away, for good.'

'Yeah, maybe.'

'Come on then,' she said quietly. 'Let's get started.'

I walked away from the studio later and thought, yeah, maybe that was it. Tel had just got out and gone, far away.

Then I remembered what Cal said. Tel had needed money, urgently. And the police said money was missing from his home. That's what happened. When he'd drawn a blank with Cal, he'd sneaked home, robbed his dad and taken off. What's stealing when you're a professional liar?

But where had he gone? The nearest airport was twenty miles away and I didn't rate searching round there. Where would I start? I'd been to the station with Tel's picture. But then I'd only asked the ticket-office people. They only see a face for a minute, through the grille. But how about the porters? They watch people hanging about. They get a better view.

It was a forlorn hope. But what was I doing the rest of the day? I strolled on down to the station and

I was already on the approach slope when I heard this voice calling. 'Hey, Jock. Hang about, lad.'

There was Porter with his bundle of mags, his face and beard like the sun setting.

'Oh, hi, Porter.'

'Sorry shouting after you like that, lad. Couldn't remember your name.'

'John.'

'Right, John. Listen. Remember that pal of yours? After we talked I asked round the caff. One of the drivers remembered him. Yeah, he did. He does a run to London every week. It was round the time you spoke to me. This kid hitched a lift, gave him a ten, seemed to have a wad in his back pocket. Dropped him off near King's Cross.'

'Get away.'

'That's it, John.'

'Thanks, Porter.'

He gave me a *Big Issue*. I gave him two quid.

'Keep the change, Porter.'

'You're a gent, Johnny.'

I walked back home with that song in my head: 'Out of that house, out of that street, and out, out of that town.'

Twenty-two

I went home that evening, had my supper, climbed the stairs to my room and lay down on the bed. Porter was right then. Tel had gone for good, like hundreds of others, down the drain into London, and if everything they said was true, he wouldn't be coming up again.

The truth had done for Tel and that was a fact. All his stories about his marvellous family, his mother spoiling him, his world tour, karate, artist-lover, they were all in his head. His real life he just couldn't bear.

Was it his stepmother going that triggered it off? She wasn't much of a mother, except in his head, not from what I'd seen. I got the feeling she despised him. What do you do if your mother despises you? You'd know, wouldn't you? How do you live? Would it have been different if she'd been different? Or was Tel just despicable? Some of the blokes thought so. They only listened to him for a giggle, to see what he'd dream up next.

But I always felt I was stuck with him. I suppose Lumber was the same, though why I can't think. He never actually helped you, did you a favour. He knew things. If you stuck around you could pick up things from him. But so?

So why had I spent most of my holidays looking for Tel? Waste of time. Well, no, it wasn't. It'd been interesting. I'd actually enjoyed the poking around. And I'd met Glenda, now that was something. And Lumber had got to join the Paras – when he was seventeen and a half.

The thought made me laugh out loud.

Everything I'd done these past weeks had been because of Tel. And still the trail had gone cold on me. He'd vanished – out of that street, that town. Now I thought of it, he'd done us more good, Lumber and me, by clearing off than he ever had sticking around.

There was a knock on the door. It was Dad.

'Are you OK, Johnny?'

'Yeah, Dad, why?'

I rolled off the bed. He came in and sat down. 'You had your supper, didn't say a word. Just went upstairs. Then we heard you laughing. I thought, the poor boy's off his trolley.'

He was joking but he was worried. I felt embarrassed.

'Cal rang,' he said. 'Told us you'd been to see him, asking about this friend. He thought it a bit strange.'

I shook my head. 'Nah, Dad, honest. I was just messing about. Playing detective.'

'Did you find out anything?'

'Not a lot. But I know he's cleared off to London with that cash he nicked from his dad. Don't suppose he'll be seen again.'

'That was a drastic thing to do.'

'Well, anyway, his stepmother was rotten to him.'

'How d'you know that, Johnny?'

'Well, that's how she seemed to me when I spoke to her.'

'Don't judge people too hastily, son.' Dad paused and looked at me. I felt he was embarrassed. 'John, if you're fed up at home, you'll tell us, won't you? We just tend to assume things are all right, if they seem like it.'

I gawped at him. ''Course they're all right, Dad. I mean, what do I have to worry about? I've got this pad and four square meals a day . . .'

He laughed. 'All right, all right. But like with your friend, things may not be what they seem. I'd like to think you'd tell us what's going on, the truth, no matter how bad it is.'

I looked past Dad. I couldn't meet his eyes. I knew things about Sis and Cal which maybe he and Mum didn't. Something flashed across my mind which helped me change the subject.

'Hey, Dad, can I ask you something?'

''Course, Johnny. How much?'

'Stop messing about, Dad. I've got this word "Amontillado" on my mind . . .'

'That's sherry, son.'

'I know, Dad, but it's not just the word. It's like a sentence with Amontillado in it.'

He thought a while, then said, 'You don't mean "The Cask of Amontillado", do you, Johnny? That horror story by Edgar Allan Poe.'

'You are brilliant, Dad. Mr Robinson read it to us at college. I remember now. It's really frightening. One bloke traps another, bricks him up in this hole in a wall and leaves him . . .'

'That's it, Johnny. Never liked it.' Then he looked at me. 'What's up, Johnny?'

I'd remembered something else. It was in class that day. Everybody was awestruck by that story, but Tel, now Tel, he had a weird look on his face. He was dead white; though he's often pale, this was worse. He was scared too, but there was something sort of eager about his face. I looked away from him and the memory of it had faded – until now.

'Well, if I'd known it was going to upset you, I wouldn't have told you,' said Dad.

'It's OK, honest. Just something I thought of. Thanks, Dad – for everything.'

He reached out, ruffled my hair and walked out of the room. It was getting dark and suddenly I felt very tired. Without getting undressed, I rolled back on to the bed and went to sleep.

I was in this town at night, everywhere pitch black, narrow streets that turned and twisted. I was heading somewhere, but the more I walked and ran and climbed over walls and jumped down piles of rubble, the further away I seemed to be from where I was going. Tel was there somewhere in the darkness, but always out of sight. I had this feeling that if I didn't find him, something dire would happen.

The craziest thing of all was, as I walked and ran, I had this one-pound coin in my hand. I held it so tight, the edge cut into me. It was important and it had something to do with Tel, but I could not say what.

I'd climbed to the top of a tall, ruined building, with brickwork flaking and crumbling. Just when I reached the top, I slipped. I began to slide down faster and faster until I hit the ground with a great jarring shock. I was awake, feet on the bed, head and shoulders on the floor. I pulled myself up, got undressed and fell into bed again.

But it was a long time before I got back to sleep.

Twenty-three

Now that Tel had definitely gone from town, the thought of him vanished too, into that inside part of my mind. It wasn't just that Tel wasn't there any more. Suddenly I had other things on my mind – one after another.

The first couple of days were great – mornings in the studio with Glenda, sitting looking out at the view, drinking coffee, chatting, looking at her when she wasn't looking at me.

Afternoons I was on my bike, riding round with Lumber, who'd suddenly resurfaced. He wanted exercise, needed to keep fit. We rode for miles, out on the moors in the sun. At first he insisted on riding up hills, to strengthen his leg muscles. I got off and pushed. After a while, though, he eased down. We'd dump the bikes on the verge and lie there looking up at the sky. The heatwave went on: the grass was turning yellow, the little streams were drying up. People were moaning about water shortage, but for us – it could go on for ever.

I came down to earth at last. Glenda told me, 'That's it, Mack. I shan't need any more sittings. I think I've got you now.'

'Hey.' I jumped. 'Can I look?'

'You cannot. There's loads of work to do, fine-tuning, which I'll do when I'm in the mood. But I'll tell you when it's done. You can look at it then.'

'Great,' I said. 'Can we celebrate?'

She gave me a funny look, then smiled. 'We'll see. You may not like it. You thought Tel's picture was weird, didn't you?'

'I never said it was weird.'

''Course you didn't, you just thought it. You can't fool me, Johnny Macklin. I know you too well.'

After that, the days started to drag. Nothing to do in the mornings. And Lumber and I ran out of places to bike to. I started to slope round town again. I'd walk past the health shop and look up at the studio window. But there was no sign of Glenda. I told myself that I was dead keen to see that finished portrait, but I knew that was rubbish. I was just dead keen to see Glenda. A couple of evenings I looked into the Green Dragon, dead casually. The barman gave me what Dad calls an old-fashioned look and I backed out again.

I looked her up in the book and more than once I went to a pay phone to dial her number, then gave up.

Once I even got through. But as she said, 'Hello', I put the phone down, feeling totally stupid.

Next day I got a grip on myself. I bought a box of chocolates, changed my shirt and walked round to the studio. I'd call on her, just casual: 'Couldn't resist asking if the picture was ready.' For ten minutes I hung about on the other pavement. I walked round the market square, then I came back, went up the stairs two at a time, gave the usual double-knock on the red and yellow door and walked in.

It was like running into a wall. She was standing by the easel pointing to something. By her side, one arm round her shoulder, was a bloke. No, not a bloke – brother Cal.

I slammed the door, more or less fell down the stairs and ran out on to the pavement. Then I charged like a maniac along the street and out into the main road. Brakes squealed and I got this mouthful of abuse from a driver. I leapt back on to the pavement.

But it made me stop and get my head together. Because I suddenly remembered what Glenda had said about Tel being boring, dropping round with flowers and chocolates. I felt a total waste of space.

I don't know what I expected, but I got more than I bargained for. My own brother picking up on his college romance. And the worst was, I'd put him up to it. I mean, I'd told him about Glenda. How stupid can you get?

I had to do something to get rid of this feeling of being an idiot. I let my feet do the thinking for me, started walking, and after about ten minutes I found myself in the street where my sister lived.

Looking at the chocolates still clutched in my hand, I thought, well, I could do the uncle bit, couldn't I? I hadn't talked to Debbie and the twins in ages.

After all, what my family did with their private lives wasn't really my business, was it? I'd drop in, have a cup of tea with Sis, as if nothing had happened. So I crossed the road and went in.

Twenty-four

It *was* as if nothing had happened. Sis was sitting at the kitchen table, Debbie on her knee, while she turned the pages of a book with her free hand. The twins were playing some game on the floor. They left it when they saw me, shouting, 'Uncle Mack', and threw themselves at my knees like Welsh full-backs.

'Let your uncle go,' said Sis, 'so he can put the kettle on.'

I put the chocolates down, filled the kettle and got the biscuit tin out and fought my way back to the table through my nephews and nieces. Sis smiled at me.

'You know, Johnny, you surprised me.'

'Eh?' I looked at her.

'Didn't realize you'd reached the age of discretion.'

'Give over. What're you on about?'

'Well, Johnny, you remember the last time you were here?'

Did I not?

'I thought you'd go straight home and tell Mum that Wally was off work.'

Wally was off work? I was getting confused. Then light dawned. That 'bloke' I'd half seen in the front room, then, was her husband. But why had she closed the door? The fog was drifting round my head again.

Sis called out. 'Tea's up, love. Johnny's here.' The inner door opened and Wally came through. He's tall and thin, but now he looked thinner, paler.

'Hi, Johnny.' He squeezed into the table and collected the kids from round my knees.

Sis poured out and turned to me again.

'The thing was, Wally was home because he'd been sacked.'

'Suspended, love,' said Brother-in-law with a wry look at me.

'Same difference.' Sis moved on. I could see she was angry, though not with us. 'They sent him home because of a mix-up in the stores, figures didn't add up. There was nothing wrong really. But they took the chance to get him out of the place.'

'Hey, what for?'

'Because there was an inquiry going on about misuse of drugs, dressings, treatment, patients, everything. Wally had set it off. He'd blown the whistle. He was so outraged about what was going on.'

'All right, all right, love,' Bro-in-law was getting embarrassed, but you couldn't stop Sis.

'I was so mad I could spit. The bloke who suspended him was up to his elbows in it. He thought that with our Wally out of the way he could bluff his way through. And at first it looked as though he'd do it too.'

'Thing is,' Wally got his oar in at last, 'it's OK

now. I've been reinstated, with full pay. It'll all come out. It was worth it, in the long run.'

Sis came in again. 'It didn't look all right at the time – no money coming in. Do you know what the mortgage is on this place, our Johnny? And it was so unjust.'

The colour came up in her cheeks. The kids' eyes were round. I reckoned they must have seen their mum in this mood more than once, these past weeks.

I spoke without thinking. 'Don't know why you wanted to keep it quiet, our Sis. You know Bro would have helped you with cash. He would, honest.' I looked at Wally. 'Though he reckons you wouldn't ask him 'cause you don't rate the way he makes his dosh.'

Sis looked astonished. I suppose the idea of her little brother and Cal discussing her affairs was a bit of a conversation-stopper. But Wally chuckled.

'You know, Johnny, Cal's more popular than he thinks. Maybe he's just guilty about being filthy rich. But the only thing I can't stand about your big brother is his habit of second-guessing everyone. I suppose it's the trade.'

'Anyway, Johnny.' Sis got her voice back. 'We wouldn't have gone to Cal and it's not what you think, or he thinks. It's, well, pride. I didn't want anybody to think we couldn't cope.'

'But does anybody include Mum and Dad then?'

''Course it does, Johnny. We didn't want them to worry. They've got enough to worry about . . .' She stopped and gave me a strange look.

I jumped in with both feet. 'Oh, come on, Sis. I know they worry a bit about people who don't pay Dad. I often hear them talking about it, when they think I'm not listening. But,' I laughed, 'Mum usually sorts it out if Dad won't.'

'No, it's not bills I meant.' Sis was embarrassed now.

'Well, what is it then?'

'She took a deep breath. 'Sometimes, our Johnny, you are gormless. It's you.'

'Me?'

'Yes, you, you idiot. They worry about you all the time.'

'Me! They never said. Anyway, what is there to worry about?'

'Well,' Sis's voice became sharper. 'They've always been a bit soft on you. Our little afterthought, they called you. I was fifteen, Cal was ten when you arrived. They always let us know what they expected from us – hard work, do well at school – and we did. But they just let you trundle along as if tomorrow was next year. And you came up to expectations.'

My mouth opened but nothing came out.

'You don't seem to worry whether you get a job when you leave school or not . . .'

'Oh, give the lad a break, Jenny,' said Wally, 'the country's not awash with jobs for school-leavers and worrying doesn't change that.'

Sis hadn't done yet. 'Well, he hasn't even got a job for the holidays.'

'I have,' I burst out.

'Oh, yes, what?'

'Never you mind.'

Wally started to laugh, then covered his mouth with his hand.

'You've got to admit, our Johnny –' Sis's voice was friendly again – 'it's a bit odd the way you've been going on these holidays, running around like a bloodhound after this mate of yours. I mean, the things you got up to.'

'How do you know what I've got up to?' Now my voice was rising, and I could see from the corner of my eye that one of the twins looked as though he was going to start skriking. So I came down the scale a note or two. 'How do you know?'

'Because you left these sheets of paper all over the place, that's how. "What I Remember", "How I Remembered It". Mum couldn't help seeing them.'

I said nothing. Cal talking to Dad. Mum talking to Sis. The bush telegraph going bongo-bongo and I hadn't a clue. Sis looked at me, then put her hand across the table and squeezed mine.

'Sorry, our Johnny. I didn't mean to go on at you like that. But you do see what I mean. It's almost as if finding this lad is more important to you than your own family.'

I got to my feet. 'I'm off.'

'Oh, I'm sorry,' Sis began.

But I shook my head. 'Nah, it's not that, Sis. I just want to think about what you said, about me and Mum and Dad. See you. See you, Wally. Glad you got your job back.'

I gave the kids a hug and stood by the kitchen door. 'Anyway, I'm not looking for Tel any more. He's gone to London – for good.'

But I was wrong, dead wrong. As I walked down the High Street I heard this banging. Nick was knocking on the caff window. I turned and went in.

He leaned over the counter. 'Your pal. The crafty little one, right?'

I stared. 'Tel, you mean?'

'Right. I seen him.'

'You what?'

'Yeah. Came in here Friday evening, asked for a burger. Started eating it as soon as I gave it him as if he was starving.'

'What did he say?'

'Nowt. Ran out without paying.'

I put my hand in my pocket and gave him two quid. 'How did he look?'

Nick gave me my change, thought a minute. 'He was dirty, clothes as if he'd slept in them, black marks on his face.'

'Black marks?'

'Yeah, like coal dust.'

'Coal dust?'

'That's right. Coal.'

Twenty-five

Coal?

Coal!

I walked away from the caff, then I started to run. I almost jumped in the air. Then I slowed down as though the effort of remembering and thinking about what I'd remembered were weighing on me, dragging at me.

But there it came, out of the dark part of my head into the open part, a stream of memories just from that one word, 'coal' – the sight of it, the feel of it, the smell of it. It was as if all those doors in the corridor opened at once and the lights went on.

I saw a street, a house, a pavement. I was kneeling on the pavement – kneeling!

> A street with no name
> A park with no trees
> A house with no windows
> A kid with no future.

But where was it? I knew and yet I couldn't say where. I was walking, running, walking and remembering, and my memories were pulling me along as if I was on the end of a lead. But where was I going?

Then I knew. I was going to school, yeah, to school, not college, not the compo, but junior school seven long years ago. I didn't need to look where I was going – I didn't need to because my feet knew the way. My attention was on the film running through my head – showing me school and the time I first met Tel.

I thought he was a creep. He was always so clean, with white shirts and a tie, looking as though he couldn't do anything wrong. And the first day he told everybody in the schoolyard, 'My name's Terrance, with an A and two Rs.'

And swot? He could tell you what seventeen elevens were without thinking. He could recite yards of poetry without looking at the book. And crafty? You wouldn't chuckle. Always working out little tricks for other people to get up to. And if it went wrong, he looked innocent with those blue eyes. He never got found out. I was the only one who saw through him – at first.

Just after he started in our class, we had story-writing. 'Write about "Where I live",' Miss told us. Everybody got their heads down. Inside five minutes, some were looking out of the window, or trying to see what their mates were writing, or chewing the end of their pencils. Some wrote half a page, then ran out of puff, like me. But not our Tel. He went on writing with a smarmy little smile on his face.

Miss smiled at him. 'Oh, Terrance, your house sounds just like those places in the estate agent's window.'

'Oh, yes, Miss,' he went, quick as a flash. 'It *was* up for sale, but it's been taken off the market. My father says it didn't reach its reserve price.'

Miss smiled even more and got him to read some out. I've forgotten most of it, but it was a load of old toffee like: 'We live in an old style end-of-terrace town house, built when Queen Victoria was on the throne. It has four spacious floors, at least ten bedrooms and three bathrooms, all en suite – from attic with dormer windows to the basement and old-fashioned sub-pavement fuel store. In a quiet cul-de-sac, it overlooks one of the city parks.'

You wouldn't believe it. But it was amazing the way the rest of the class lapped it up.

Then holidays. Tel didn't go on about boring Costa del Sol or Torremewheresit. Not him. Some place called Aberhof, 'known as the Austrian Riviera,' he said.

Nobody checked up on him, of course. And you couldn't check up where he lived, because every afternoon he disappeared up School Lane like a puff of smoke.

'Got to rush,' he'd say. 'Dad'll be waiting for me with the limo.'

'Why doesn't he pick you up outside school like everybody else?' I asked him.

He looked at me as if I was two screws short of a box. 'Oh, no. This road's too narrow. He'd go spare if the bodywork got scratched. My dad's very, very fussy.'

But he got worse. One day we were talking about

life-saving. There'd been a crash on the M4 and this bloke had risked his life pulling people out of the wreckage.

Miss told us, 'There's an old Chinese proverb that if you save someone, they owe you their life for ever after and you're responsible for them.'

We all chewed that one over, except Tel. He had his hand up in a flash. 'My dad says you have to be careful about helping other people. You might do more harm than good.'

Miss gave him a funny look. 'Why's that, Terrance?'

Tel looked round to make sure we were all listening. Of course we were.

'There was this bloke rode pillion on his mate's motorbike. It was freezing cold, midwinter. So he took off his coat and put it on back to front and got his friend to fasten it at the back, to keep the wind off his chest when they were driving along. Going round a bend at seventy, the road was like glass. The bike skidded across the road and the passenger fell off. By the time the biker stopped and got back, there was a crowd round his mate. "Is he all right?" he asked. "Yes," they told him. "When we found your friend his head was twisted round back to front. But we've put that right now."'

Everybody was silent. Miss put her hand to her mouth.

'Did that really happen, Terrance?' she asked.

'Oh, yes,' said Tel. 'It was on the news.'

One or two people looked a bit doubtful. So I

put the boot in. 'I watch *Newsround* regularly. I've never seen anything like that.'

He didn't even blink. 'Not English news – Spanish news. We get it by satellite.'

Afterwards, in the schoolyard, everybody gathered round Tel. He was giving them all the details about this super satellite dish.

'My dad has a special decoder. You can't buy them in this country, not even for a thousand pounds,' he said. 'It even translates for you.'

Everybody gawped. It sounded fantastic. Who could tell?

Every day at break-time after that, there was this little crowd round him, listening to Spanish satellite news.

I could have spit.

Tel knew I didn't reckon much to him. But he was always trying to get round me, calling me Macker and looking at me while he was spinning his yarns.

But I didn't trust him.

He played a trick on Lumber. That was his nickname even then, always scowling and saying, 'You wait till break, you're in dead lumber, right?'

Crafty little Tel put somebody up to sticking a Post-it label on Lumber's back, saying 'Mr Blobby' or some rubbish like that. Lumber walked round with it on for ten minutes, trying to work out why all the class was having a giggle. I'd have taken it off, only I was scared he might blame me.

Who told him? Of course, it was Tel.

After Lumber had been traipsing round looking

stupid for most of the break, Tel shouts out, 'You are a rotten lot, laughing at Gary. No, it's not fair. I'll take it off.'

He made Gary stop, then put on a big show of pulling the notice off and ripping it up.

'Who did that?' demanded Lumber. 'They're in dead lumber if I find out.'

'No idea,' said Tel, his eyes big and round. 'But I'll tell you something for nothing, it wasn't me.'

It wasn't either, not much.

After that Tel and Lumber started going around together. But I noticed that Tel still went off home by himself. Even his best friends weren't getting to see his town house and his dad's limo.

I don't know why Tel needled me, but he did. I should really have scrubbed round the little nerd. The trouble was, he wouldn't leave me alone.

We were doing quiet reading one afternoon. I was deep into this story. Somebody nudged me. Tel was sliding a note across to me. I was so surprised I jumped.

That made Miss look up just as Tel's hand pushed something into mine. But quick as light he whispered very loudly, 'No, thanks, Macker,' and shoved my hand away with the note in it.

I tried to hide it, but Miss was there, beckoning. Of course, she thought I was trying to pass the note to him. Nothing I could say beat that innocent look on his little face.

'This is disgusting, John,' she told me. And I hadn't even seen what was in it. What was worse, she made a big deal of the whole business, not her usual way, which was giving you a very quiet, deadly little telling-off by her desk, so you could choose whether you told anyone else what it was all about or not.

I was choked. By the end of the afternoon steam was coming out of my ears. Tel knew. He took off like a rocket after school, but I was faster. Then, just as I was about to destroy him, who should come up but big Gary.

'You leave our Tel alone or you're in dead lumber, right?' he said, sticking his sausage finger into my chest. 'Right?'

Right.

But now I had made my mind up that I was going to sort Terrance out. And the best way I could think of was to find out the real story, the truth about all this rubbish, town house, limo, super satellite dish. Then I'd make him look stupid.

Well, I did find out, and quickly. The funny thing was, some of it was true . . . sort of.

Suddenly I was in School Lane. It was empty – holiday time. And anyway, it was late afternoon. I knew that because I was dead hungry, though now I wasn't thinking of my stomach. I wasn't thinking *now* at all – I was thinking *then*.

On the wall, by the school, very faintly scrawled on the brickwork, were the words 'Tel is a roten liar'.

I'd remembered that earlier on, but couldn't say who'd written it. Now I knew. It was me.

And I knew where I had to look for Tel.

I about-faced and went back down School Lane. But I was going slowly now, as if I were shadowing someone, which I was – Tel.

Tel not *now*, but *then*. The ten-year-old Tel whose guts I hated so much.

Twenty-six

I'd been keeping Tel under surveillance. And I noticed something funny. He was looking paler. Well, he always looked a bit that way, but this was different. As though he was worried. No tricks, no bragging, no Spanish satellite stories. He was quiet, too quiet.

Then one morning he was sent for by the Head. I got myself excused, nipped out to the toilets. Half-way there, between the staff-room and the Head's office, there's a corner where the pipes run up the wall. You stand there, as if you're waiting for a teacher, and you can hear what goes on.

Today there was no problem. You could hear it all down the corridor. Tel's father was in and laying down the law. Big voice booming away. I pictured this bloke, big as a gorilla.

'One pound, madam. One pound, completely gone. Now, as you well know I am all in favour of charity collections, but to induce Terrance to give two weeks' pocket money is going too far.'

'But, Mr Holbrook,' the Head answered, 'we have not had a charity collection this term so far. Terrance . . .'

She got no further.

'Are you suggesting my son is a liar, madam?'

He sounded as though he was about to do somebody a mischief, but the Head was quite calm.

'I'm afraid that Terrance is a little inclined to romance. Perhaps he watches too much television.'

'Television?' roared Tel's dad. 'There is no such thing in our home. What gave you that impression? Terrance spends his evenings studying his timestables and his other schoolbooks.'

'I beg your pardon,' said the Head. 'Perhaps Terrance can explain.'

Not much. Tel, like those monks, had taken a vow of silence.

Then his Dad said menacingly, 'Terrance *will* explain to me when he comes home tonight. Mark my words, we shall track down the truth.'

There was a scraping sound like a chair going back. I dodged along the corridor. But I saw Tel's dad go across the yard.

He wasn't a big bloke, but stiff and straight, all in uniform, black with a peaked cap – like an official driver. So that was the limo Tel had bragged about.

Then I saw it and almost had a fit. Parked outside the school gate was a funeral car.

I could hardly wait for school to end. Everything was going my way. Mum was due to be late back from work. I had the key, with strict instructions to be home before five. That gave me all the time I needed.

When Tel, looking like death warmed up, crawled

off home, I was close behind him. But not too close. As he sloped through the back streets, I tailed him, ducking behind corners and dodging into doorways.

We were getting into the beat-up part of town, streets of old houses jammed close together to stop them falling down. As we went the roads got narrower and more bashed about. Town houses? I should coco.

At last he turned off. I had to hang back. He was bound to look round when he got home. When I finally reached the corner, Tel had vanished. The street was a dead end – a cul-de-sac, he'd called it. Across the bottom was a big wall. And I realized what was on the other side. 'Overlooking one of the city parks,' he'd said. Yes – a car park.

But he was right about the houses. They did have four floors, attic and basement, those that were still standing. Some had been pulled down, like teeth being taken out. Others were empty, the windows smashed.

The street seemed empty too as I walked along, trying to work out which place was Tel's. It wasn't all that hard to find. Right at the end of the street, the only house with curtains in all the windows and a big, torn notice saying 'For Sa –'

The front door was green. Or had been once. Now all the paint was peeling. And alongside were bell pushes, half a dozen of them. Tel's story was true. He lived in a town house with four floors. And so did twenty other people by the look of it. But which floor did Tel and his terrifying dad live on?

I soon found out.

Wandering along the street, keeping an eye open in case I was spotted, though the street was dead quiet, I suddenly heard a noise, a strange noise.

It was muffled, like someone speaking down a tunnel. Well, not speaking, sort of chanting in a desperate way. I could faintly hear the words – and recognize them.

'Eleven elevens are 121, twelve elevens are 132.' It stopped, then began again, more high-pitched:

'What is this life if, full of care,
We have no time to stand and stare?'

No mistaking that voice. It was our Tel. And weirder still, it came from underneath my feet.

I looked down. Right in the centre of the pavement was a round brass plate with a ring in it. I knew what it was, because Gran's house used to have one. It was a coal hole. People used to have their solid fuel tipped down through it, into a little place underneath, with a door just opposite the basement window.

And the sound was coming up from there. Tel had gone straight into the coal hole as soon as he reached home. Or more likely he'd been sent in there. And he was getting more and more wound up by the minute.

Suddenly I thought, he must be scared stiff in the dark and the filth, with the cobwebs and creepy-crawlies.

I glanced round. No one was in sight. The basement curtains were closed tight. Now I knelt and put my finger into the ring in the brass plate, feeling a bit like Aladdin – only this wasn't a treasure chamber, it was a prison.

Giving a good tug, I almost fell over as the plate came up. With it came a smell of old dust, coal, bad earth. It was horrible. Below was dead silence now, but just a little way below me Tel's face looked up, white in the light. He'd been crying, his face was all teary.

'Macker!'

He looked as if he'd like to vanish. But no luck. There was nowhere to go. I guessed he was due to stay there till he'd finished his prison term.

'Tel,' I whispered. 'Your dad put you in here, didn't he?'

He nodded. No smart answers now. I was getting the truth and nothing but the truth.

'Just for a quid?'

Silence, then, 'How did you know that?'

'Never mind. I know a lot about you, Tel.' I was enjoying this – a bit. 'One pound is two weeks' pocket money, isn't it?'

'Yes,' his voice squeaked.

'And your dad's making you stay here. No tea, I bet.'

'I don't get out till I tell him what I did with it.'

'You nana. Why didn't you say you lost it?'

'He wouldn't believe me.'

Oh, yes, that was how it was. Tel had to tell the truth at home. Or else.

'So what *did* you do with it?'

He didn't answer for a minute. Then he looked up. His tears had dried but his nose was running. 'I gave it to Lumber. I thought you were going to duff me up.'

My mouth fell open, then I had to laugh. 'Stupid! Stupid! I was mad with you but . . . You know, Tel, you ought to have more common. You're a rotten fibber, aren't you? You should give it up. You're not really any good at it, are you?'

He said nothing. But suddenly I wasn't mad with him any more. I was just sorry for him. I fished in my pocket, pulled out a squashed half-Mars Bar and dropped it down. He caught it and made it vanish somewhere inside his shirt, like a conjuring trick.

'Look, Tel, I'm putting the lid on, right? I'll talk to your dad.'

'Hey, don't!'

'Don't worry, I won't tell him the truth. I'll think of some story.'

I put the lid on, climbed to my feet and went down the steps. As I reached the bottom the basement door slammed. Tel's dad was glaring down at me.

'What are you doing there, lad?'

'Looking for Tel . . . I mean Terrance, Mister.'

'What for?'

I held up my hand with a pound coin in it. My week's pocket money. Twice what Tel got, but all I had.

'Terrance lost this, Mister. I found it under his desk after he went home.'

He looked at me, like a stoat sizing up a rabbit. 'Is that the truth?'

I was ready for that. I stared back, eyes wide. ''Course, Mister.'

He climbed the stairs and took the coin. Not a word. No thank-you. Nothing.

Now the memory film came to an end. I didn't need to see any more. I didn't want to see any more.

I knew why I'd been looking for Tel. It was like Miss said all those years ago, the old Chinese saying: You save someone once and you're responsible for them for ever.

Twenty-seven

I stopped dead in my tracks. This was the street, I knew that. But it had changed. No, not changed, vanished. There was nothing there. On either side, all the way down, as far as the high wall that hid the car park, there was empty space: no houses, just piles of raw pink and brown brick, smashed window-frames and here and there chunks of wall with the faded flowered wallpaper still stuck on them. The whole lot had been knocked down.

My legs had lost their strength. I could not move. Had I got it all wrong after all? But I knew I was in the right place, the street with no name. Tel had to be here. I made my legs move and slowly I drew nearer to the wall, where I knew Tel's house had been.

And it *was* there. The last mound of rubble, then, like a ditch, the gap next to the pavement where the steps down into the basement had been. Right in front of me the rubbish on the pavement had been pushed aside and the brass circle in the middle of the paving stones had been brushed clear.

I was kneeling on the ground again, a chunk of wood in my hand, levering up the brass plate, when I stopped and stood up, my stomach like ice. From my position on the pavement I could look over the edge into the basement area. Down below me the bottom was piled with bricks, heaped up against the old coal-house door. They must have fallen from the great pile where the main house had been. Anyone behind that door would be trapped.

Trembling, I knelt down again, groping for the wood I'd dropped. I wedged the point into the brass ring and levered upwards. It came easily. The black hole below me opened up and, as it did, a rush of air hit me in the face. It was putrid: stale food, sweat, worse, and behind that this old, old coal smell.

'Tel,' I whispered, 'are you down there?'

No answer, but I had this crazy feeling that it wasn't empty. It didn't sound, it didn't feel, empty. Gritting my teeth, I stretched my hand and arm down through the opening, into the darkness. My spread-out fingers touched something. I groaned, jerked away, then forced my fingers to reach out again. This time they told me what it was — hair, someone's head.

'Tel — are you . . .'

The head lolled away out of my grasp.

Twenty-eight

I got to my feet, still shaking, and staggered off down the street to the nearest payphone. I'm not going to explain what I did next. I didn't ring 999. I didn't ring home. I rang Lumber. For a miracle, he was in.

'Yeah, Mack. You were lucky, mate. I was on my way out.'

'Listen, Gary.'

'What's up?' He must have caught the hysteria in my voice.

'Remember you owe me one?'

There was a silence.

'Ye-es. Listen, Mack, if this is about finding Tel, then forget it. I told you –'

'I know what you told me, Gary. It's not about finding Tel. I've found him.'

'You what?'

'I've found him, but –'

'But what, Mack?

'I'm not sure – how he is.'

Another silence.

'Where are you?'

Where was I? If this street has a name, it had no name plate.

'Gary, you know Brewergate?'

'That dump?'

'Yeah. You know Calder Road?'

'Think so.'

'Right. Third turning on right. Down at the bottom up against the car park. And Gary – there's no houses.'

'What is this, Mack?'

'Gary – you owe me.'

'OK, OK. I'll be there in twenty minutes.'

'And Gary, come in your old clothes and – bring a shovel.'

'You're out of your box. This sounds like big trouble.'

'All right, Gary. If that's how you feel . . . Don't expect too much from a trainee Para.'

'Mack, I'll tear your head off.'

'You'll have to come round here first.'

'On my way. And, Mack, I just hope we don't regret this. Correction – you don't regret it.'

When Lumber makes his mind up, he doesn't hang about. He was down with me in ten minutes – got a taxi, shovel and all, and came rolling down the pavement, eyes taking in the ruins on either side.

I didn't speak, just pointed to the hole in the pavement and then to the basement area. He bent over, caught a whiff from below, stared at me, then, without a word, lowered himself into the old basement area and went to work.

For half an hour – though it felt much longer – we worked. Lumber passed up lumps of brick and I hurled them up on to the main pile. My hands were cut and bruised and filthy. Lumber was in a worse state, but he said nothing, only grunted and strained down there.

At last came the scrape of the shovel. Dust and small bits of brick came flying out of the pit.

'Get down here, Mack,' he called.

I dropped into the area. That was clear. But behind, where the basement door and window had been, was bulging with rubble.

'That stuff's going to shoot out any minute, I reckon,' whispered Lumber. 'Come on.' He shoved the blade of the shovel into the edge of the coal-house door and heaved. The rotten wood splintered and fell away.

Tel's body slumped sideways into our arms. We gulped at the smell of him. Lumber signalled to me. I climbed out and he hoisted the body up. There wasn't much weight. There never had been, but these last few days he must have starved.

I dragged off my T-shirt, rolled it up and put it under Tel's head, where he lay on the pavement. The face under its streaks of coal dust was dead white, the long eyelashes looked as if they had mascara on them.

'Poor little sod.' Lumber was standing over me where I knelt by Tel's side. 'What do we do now?'

'Do? Dunno. I suppose we're forced to tell his dad.'

Tel's head moved. At first I thought it was just falling to one side. But no, now it moved the other way. The head was shaking – as if he was saying. 'No.'

His eyes are incredibly blue, I thought. Why? 'Cause they were open. He was looking at me and shaking his head.

'I don't believe it,' said Lumber. 'He's alive!'

Twenty-nine

We got Tel to Lumber's place – his mother was weekending with Sergeant Harris. Tel could just about walk, hanging on to us. He was weak from hunger and thirst, but he wouldn't let us call an ambulance or a taxi. No one must know. We thought he was crazy – but it was his life.

Once we were there, Lumber and I divided the work up. I took Tel up to the bathroom and helped him clean up. He was like a baby. Afterwards I cleaned the bathroom (if Mum could have seen me on my knees!) and his clothes I stuffed in a plastic bag and shoved them outside the back door. Then, a pair of Lumber's pyjamas, with the sleeves and legs rolled up and he was sitting, well half lying, in one of the armchairs downstairs eating the pizzas that Lumber had collected and drinking the tea he'd brewed.

After a while, when he was convinced we weren't going to let his father know we'd found him, he began to talk. Some of it I already knew or could guess. Lumber had no idea, and to say he was gobsmacked does not begin to describe it.

But he knew and I knew – and this was the funny thing about it, though the story was more incredible than any he had told us in the past – it was true. It poured out of him for nearly an hour, with bites of pizza and drinks of tea.

His mother had died when he was so small, he only had the vaguest of memories, like dreams. From then on until three years ago, when his Dad married again, they'd been on their own. There was no getting away from his father, except when he went to school. And even then he felt his dad was watching him.

Every afternoon when he got home, his father would be there back from a funeral in his black suit. That terrified him. Next would come the questions. What had he learned? What had he done? Had he been praised? How many gold stars had he got? Had he been – in trouble? 'Tell the truth, Terrance, you must always tell the truth.' His dad would go on at him until he didn't know what was the truth and what was something he'd make up to buy time. It made no difference. The end was always the same.

'The worst was when he shook me,' said Tel. 'You feel your insides are coming loose.'

Then he was sent out to the coal hole and the door shut. It could only be opened from outside. For an hour, sometimes more, he would sit in the dark, with things crawling all over him.

He would try to remember the things he was supposed to know or the 'truth' he was supposed to tell, or try to work himself up to saying sorry for whatever it was he was supposed to have done wrong.

But there was worse. When he was in bed. He

was always sent up to bed, then his dad would come in and sit beside him in the dark.

'He'd always say, "Now, dads and sons must be friends, mustn't they? Dads and sons are friends, aren't they?" Then . . .'

Tel started to cry. We watched him, speechless. Lumber fetched him a handkerchief and he started talking again, but he couldn't finish.

'What about your stepmother?' I asked.

He shook his head. 'I thought she'd change things. I thought it'd change when he got promoted and we moved to a new house out at Framleigh.'

But it didn't. His dad got even more obsessed with what people would think about the family. Tel must not let his father down.

Lumber stared at Tel. 'Look, couldn't you even tell your stepmother what was going on?'

Tel stared back as if Lumber was an idiot. 'She wouldn't have believed me. She never believed anything I said. She – despised me.'

His work at school went to pieces. His cover-up stories developed though. They got more and more inventive. He couldn't tell what was real and what wasn't.

'I got to think there were only two ways out. I could run away. Or I'd have to kill him.'

'Kill your dad?' We both spoke together.

He started to laugh and cry at the same time. 'Do you know what I was going to do? I was going to get him down to that house and into the coal hole. Then I was going to shut him in and tumble all the bricks down and bury him alive, like in that horror story.'

'"The Cask of Amontillado",' I said in awe.

'But I never dared. When she went, I got desperate and I did a bunk. I tried to get a job. No way. They thought I was round the twist. They were right. I sneaked back home. I knew he kept money in the house. I took it and ran off again.'

He'd had a few days in London, spending. He didn't dare stay anywhere big, in case they told the police. But someone had noticed him. He was mugged and the rest of his money stolen.

So he'd crawled back – back to the street and the house – and hidden in the coal hole, like an animal. Then one night he'd heard the bricks fall down and block the door. He was trapped.

'It was what I'd been going to do to him. It was a punishment.'

'Get off.' Lumber was furious. 'Punishment. What for? Burying alive's too good for that bastard.'

'What're you going to do, Tel?' I asked.

'Don't know. But I'm not going home. Whatever he says. Whatever stories he tells.'

'Listen, Tel,' I went on. 'You've got to talk to someone. The best way you can get it right is tell other people how it's been.' I dug in my pocket and pulled out Sergeant Taylor's card. 'Tel, you've got to trust Gary and me.'

'I won't go back.'

'Trust us, Tel. If we were going to let you down, would we have come and dug you out of that place?'

'Right,' added Lumber.

I picked up the phone.

Half an hour later Sergeant Taylor and WPC Chesters arrived. She sat by Tel while he went over the whole story again. Every now and again the sergeant asked a question. This time round Tel managed to go through it without breaking down.

There was only one bad moment, when Sergeant Taylor said, 'Terrance, it is very important that you are telling us the truth.'

Tel's eyes got very big. I thought for a moment he would burst into tears. This was the bottom line. It's one thing to tell lies and get found out. But it's nothing to when you tell the truth and they won't believe you. It was like running into a brick wall. I racked my brains to think of something to say that would convince the Law.

Lumber clinched it. He went almost purple in the face and burst out, 'Do us a favour, Sergeant. You don't sit for days in a shitty coal hole for a giggle.'

WPC Chesters gave a tiny smile. Sergeant Taylor nodded. Then he signalled to her and the two of them went into the next room.

When they came back, she put a hand on Tel's shoulder. 'I'm taking you to the hospital. They may keep you there a day or two, make sure you're OK.'

Sergeant Taylor said, 'I shall have to go and talk with your father.'

Tel's face went even paler. The sergeant raised his hand. 'But you don't have to see him until we've arranged for third parties – Social people – to be present. It's going to be a bit rough, lad, but we'll sort it.'

I don't know if Tel believed him, but Lumber spoke quietly: 'We'll see you right, Tel. Trust us.'

So he went, with Lumber's pyjamas on and WPC Chesters carrying his filthy clobber in this plastic bag.

Sergeant Taylor followed them out to the car, but turned in the doorway and said to me, 'Congratulations, John. Have you ever thought of joining the Force?'

Lumber shouted with laughter.

Sergeant Taylor looked at him. 'Did I say something funny?'

'You don't know how funny, Sarge,' he answered.

Thirty

This story is not as long as that lot the French bloke wrote in bed, but it's long enough for me and it's taken me right through the holidays. Back at college tomorrow, when I'll get a real rest.

Let me put the other things down in the order they happened.

A day or two after we found Tel, a young woman came to our house. Not quite as classy as Glenda, but not bad, and nearer my age. She was from the local evening. How she knew about it all I don't know, but there are tricks to every trade, like detective work.

She was fascinated by all the stuff I'd written down. Well, she said it was fascinating, yeah and exciting. There was a big front-page story, afterwards, with a picture of Lumber and me – him holding his shovel, me with a notebook, would you believe?

'Two local heroes save pal from living tomb,' was the headline. 'Amateur sleuth tracks down missing teenager' and the rest, totally cringe-making. There was a bit about Lumber planning to join the Paras and how I looked forward to a career in journalism or the police. Now that I never said. This was news, yet was it the whole truth and nothing but the truth?

It was what journalists call a good story though.

But there was a big hole in it. Nowhere was there a word about Tel's father. And there was a very good reason for that. Sergeant Taylor had seen him that night and arranged to see him again the following afternoon – officially. But next day he was nowhere to be found. He'd packed his bags, cleared his bank account and vanished into thin air. As far as I know, he's on the run still, and I hope he goes on running for a long time – until he gets to feel like Tel felt. Though that I doubt.

That's not the end of it. Who should turn up again and start living in the house he'd left behind but his wife, Tel's stepmother? And she kindly invited Tel to go and live there. But Tel wasn't having it. When they let him out of hospital, he stayed with us for a while. Mum cleared out the spare room. Then they found him a place in a hostel. He's staying there till he's finished at college. After that he gets a job at Media Mark. Who fixed that? I leave you to guess.

So, that was Lumber fixed and Tel fixed. What about me?

I was in the market square yesterday. The weather had broken. It was raining and I was sheltering under the cake-shop awning.

Someone said, 'Fancy a coffee, Mack?' It was Glenda.

I didn't say a word, just followed her to the stairs by the health shop and up, past that red and yellow door, into the studio. My picture was there, standing against the wall. It took a bit of getting used to – I mean, you just don't see yourself as other people do. What can I say? It looked better than what I see in the mirror, and I don't mean she missed the spots out. It looked older somehow.

She'd painted me sitting on a hillside, looking out over the ground beneath, with a town in the distance. It was as though I'd travelled a long way and was resting before I set off again. Just how I felt.

'Like it?'

I nodded. That was simpler than speaking.

Glenda handed me a mug of coffee. 'Guess what? Cal bought it.'

'He what?'

'He did.' She gave me a quick, funny glance. 'That was why he was here that day you crashed in.'

I was about to say, 'I never crashed in,' when she went on, grinning, 'Don't suppose you kept the chocs. I don't deserve them, do I?'

Now I laughed. 'I gave them to my sister's kids.'

She must have seen another question in my face. 'I think he was after more than buying a picture. I think he fancied starting again where we left off after college, but I don't like being put down and picked up again, Johnny. I'm happy on my own for the moment.'

I looked round the studio. 'Where's Tel's picture?'

'Put away for now. One of these days, I'll have a little show – of nineties people. This mate of yours, the one who's going for a soldier, would he sit for me, d'you think?'

I thought quickly. 'I'll ask him. Tell you what, I'll bring him round, shall I?'

She smiled and said, 'Great.'

We drank our coffee, chatted about Life and the Universe, then I said, 'See ya', she gave me a kiss and I went down the stairs, down the street and off towards home. It had stopped raining and the sun was shining on the puddles.

It all seemed quite clear to me now. I could work as a journalist, or maybe join the police, or maybe not. I could even start a job agency, I was pretty hot on that, or, thinking about Sergeant Harris and Lumber's mum, a dating agency.

Or I could do something seriously boring, like passing my exams and going to university.

My real ambition, though, is to be an artist's model.

... if you liked this, you'll love these ...

BECOMING JULIA
A deadly obsession
Chris Westwood

'Julia, I didn't ask to be involved, but here I am, look at me. I'm becoming like you and there's no turning back.'

Maggie has never met Julia Broderick, the girl on the police Missing posters, but their likeness is truly uncanny. When Julia's body is fished out of the river, Maggie is drawn into the tangled web surrounding the dead girl and realizes that to uncover the truth she must first enter Julia's world. As Maggie comes closer to finding out what really happened, is she also close to sharing Julia's fate?

'Becoming Julia confirms Chris Westwood's reputation as a superior thriller writer' – *The Times*

BROTHER OF MINE
Chris Westwood

**'Do you have any brothers or sisters?' she asked.
'A brother,' I tell her. 'But you wouldn't like him, he's nothing like me at all.'**

Nick is convinced that his twin brother Tony is after everything that is his. After all, isn't Tony the one who always gets the girls, the grades and the pats on the back?

But then there is Alex, the girl at the party, and it seems at last that someone wants Nick for himself. However, when Alex mistakes Tony for Nick, Tony plays along ...

... if you liked this, you'll love these ...

LOCKED IN TIME
Lois Duncan

When seventeen-year-old Nore arrives at the old Louisiana plantation home of her father and his new wife, she is prepared for unhappiness. She did not expect her new family to be so different. Lisette, her new mother, is exotically beautiful, yet Nore senses evil. She is attracted to Lisette's son, Gabe, but why is he so bitter about life? As time passes she pieces together a strange and terrible truth about the family; Nore is a threat to their secret – and threats must be destroyed.

STRANGER WITH MY FACE
Lois Duncan

'Are you the one with my face?' I whispered.
'I came first,' she answered with a little laugh, 'It's you who have my face.'

For seventeen-year-old Laurie it has been a wonderful summer, filled with sun, sea and romance. Then the nightmare begins.

First her boyfriend breaks up with her. He insists he saw her with another boy, but Laurie knows it wasn't her. Then her friends start avoiding her because she said something she knew she hadn't.

Laurie has a chilling feeling that someone is watching her, spying on her. Someone with her face, someone with sinister intentions ...

... if you liked this book, try these ...

FALL-OUT
Gudrun Pausewang

'Your attention, please; this is the police. A nuclear accident took place about ten o'clock this morning inside the Grafenrheinfeld nuclear power station. The population of the entire district is urgently requested to move at once to a closed room and shut all doors and windows. These are precautionary measures. There is no need for anxiety . . .'

As the radioactive fall-out gets closer, the government's glib plans for coping with such a disaster collapse. Fourteen-year-old Janna, left alone to look after her little brother in a world gone mad with fear, must make the decisions which will mean life or death for both of them.

'A sobering but totally consuming novel by an excellent writer' – *Sunday Telegraph*

'Hard truths about the effects of fall-out make this book gripping, its message cannot be mistaken' – *School Library Journal*

ECHOES OF WAR
Robert Westall

Even when wars are over, they leave their mark in the minds of those who lived through them and echo down through the years. In this compelling collection of short stories by a writer who has never forgotten – and can never forget – the war he lived through, you will discover the powerful and total experience of war and its indelible scars.

READ MORE IN PUFFIN

For children of all ages, Puffin represents quality and variety – the very best in publishing today around the world.

For complete information about books available from Puffin – and Penguin – and how to order them, contact us at the appropriate address below. Please note that for copyright reasons the selection of books varies from country to country.

On the worldwide web: www.penguin.co.uk

In the United Kingdom: Please write to *Dept. EP, Penguin Books Ltd, Bath Road, Harmondsworth, West Drayton, Middlesex UB7 0DA*.

In the United States: Please write to *Penguin Putnam inc., P.O. Box 12289, Dept B, Newark, New Jersey 07101-5289* or call 1-800-788-6262

In Canada: Please write to *Penguin Books Canada Ltd, 10 Alcorn Avenue, Suite 300, Toronto, Ontario M4V 3B2*

In Australia: Please write to *Penguin Books Australia Ltd, P.O. Box 257, Ringwood, Victoria 3134*

In New Zealand: Please write to *Penguin Books (NZ) Ltd, Private Bag 102902, North Shore Mail Centre, Auckland 10*

In India: Please write to *Penguin Books India Pvt Ltd, 11 Panscheel Shopping Centre, Panscheel Park, New Delhi 110 017*

In the Netherlands: Please write to *Penguin Books Netherlands bv, Postbus 3507, NL-1001 AH Amsterdam*

In Germany: Please write to *Penguin Books Deutschland GmbH, Metzlerstrasse 26, 60594 Frankfurt am Main*

In Spain: Please write to *Penguin Books S. A., Bravo Murillo 19, 1° B, 28015 Madrid*

In Italy: Please write to *Penguin Italia s.r.l., Via Felice Casati 20, I–20124 Milano*

In France: Please write to *Penguin France S. A., 17 rue Lejeune, F–31000 Toulouse*

In Japan: Please write to *Penguin Books Japan, Ishikiribashi Building, 2–5–4, Suido, Bunkyo-ku, Tokyo 112*

In South Africa: Please write to *Longman Penguin Southern Africa (Pty) Ltd, Private Bag X08, Bertsham 2013*

That wine took your last penny more or less, didn't it? So this is important to you, right?'

I nodded.

'I rate that, John. I like people who have things that matter to them. They begin to be interesting to me.'

She stood up. I followed. She held out her hand. I grabbed it. She squeezed mine, then let go.

'Eleven o'clock tomorrow then.'

She grinned, a really broad grin, and said very quietly, 'And you can keep your kit on.'

mean like innocent, but I don't think you're stupid. Whereas your friend had a sly look.'

'Sly?' I was surprised. 'We all thought he looked so innocent he could get away with owt at school.'

She shrugged. 'Call it the artist's eye. Look, I don't mean to insult your friend, but I wouldn't have trusted him – much.'

I listened, wanting to tell her what I really thought about Tel, about knowing that wasn't what mattered.

'Why ask me about him, John?'

'He's gone missing from home and I – I wanted to find out what happened to him.'

'And you thought I might know. Look, John, it must be getting on for two months since I saw him last and there was no sign of him being on the run.'

She stopped to sip her wine, then suddenly asked, 'What did he tell you about me?'

I was silent. Something made me turn round. Other people had come into the lounge, so I lowered my voice. 'He said you picked him up here and wanted to paint him with his kit off.'

She started to laugh, then frowned and shook her head. 'Your pal is certainly economical with the truth.' She looked round. 'We can't talk properly in this place. I tell you what. Can you come to my place tomorrow, like eleven? I've got a studio over the health shop at the corner of Ryder Street.'

She squeezed up her eyes. 'I think I'd like to do a few sketches of you. I'll pay you modelling time, say five quid an hour.' She caught the look on my face and added, 'I know you're short of cash, John.

fellers do that to me, I usually let them know they're a waste of space. I don't want you to think I'm anybody's for a glass of Muscadet.'

The words rushed out of my mouth. 'I wasn't trying to pick you up.'

'Well, for someone who isn't trying, you're a fast mover. What are you like when you make an effort?'

'No.' I had to get out of this cross-talk act before I said something stupid. 'I wanted to ask you something, Glenda.'

'All right. But first tell me something. How do you know my name? And how come you made your pitch ten seconds after I came in tonight? What's going on, John? Were you waiting for me? I'm not sure I like that.'

I was suddenly angry. 'Listen. I didn't mean to sound cheeky. But there is something you might be able to tell me. Seriously.'

'This is for real, isn't it, John?' She was looking at me steadily now. 'But what can I tell you? I don't even know you. How come you know me?'

'I don't, honest. Never seen you before. It's my mate Tel, Terrance Holbrook.'

I passed over the photo. She smoothed it out and frowned, then nodded. Then she looked carefully at me.

'He's your mate, John? Well, it takes all sorts. But you are so different from him.'

'How d'you mean, Glenda?' I was using her name more easily now.

'Don't be offended, but you look a bit naive, I

84

Eighteen

Her laugh lasted about two or three seconds. But in that time everybody in the bar turned round. My face went red. Hot flushes ran down to my ankles. I wanted to run out of the pub, but I couldn't move.

Then she stopped laughing and said, 'Yes, why not? I'll have a white wine.'

It took every penny I had left in my pocket, bar a five-pence piece.

She gave me a quick glance then said, 'Aren't you having anything – ?'

'John,' I gabbled. 'Mine's over there.' I jerked my head towards the corner, hoping the bar staff hadn't taken my glass, which still had some warm cider in it.

Her eye followed mine. My place had been grabbed already.

'Let's go in the snug, John.'

I followed her and felt my breathing go back to normal.

We sat down. She raised her glass.

'Thanks, John. Good luck.'

I raised my glass. I began to wish people *were* looking at me now.

'I'll tell you something for nothing, John. When

And there I was in the Green Dragon. That existed all right. But as for a middle-aged artist with a taste for teenage boys . . .

'Good evening, Glenda.'

The barman's voice reached me through all the din. Standing at the bar so close I could almost lean out and touch her was this woman. She wasn't nearly forty. Just comparing her face with my sister's, I could tell she wasn't even thirty. She was slim and dressed in jeans with a long shirt spattered with paint. Her face, in profile, with these dark curls, was – well – lovely.

I was standing next to her. I don't remember getting up. She turned. Her eyes were oval and a bit slanting, almost Japanese. She smiled as if she was waiting for me to talk to her.

So I said the first thing that came into my head – the inside part. 'Can I buy you a drink, Glenda?'

She stared. Then she laughed out loud.

I could have died.

you in the nude." So – he got his kit off and you
know what? She painted these stripes down his back.
Then she got him to turn round and – oh, mate . . .'

'Listen,' I said, 'I do not even believe Tel said
that.'

'Why d'you reckon?'

'Because,' I said patiently, 'Tel's stories are more
or less believable.' I had to say that. 'What I mean
is, they sound true. That one sounds rubbish.'

Rick shrugged. 'What's the difference, Macker –
a lie you believe or one you can't?'

'I mean one is truer than the other.'

'Truer?' Now they were both laughing.

'What I mean is –' I was trying to make sense of
this – 'if you are going to find out what Tel is up
to, you have to know how much truth there is in
his lies.'

They stopped laughing.

'But we're not trying to find him,' said Rick. 'I've
scrubbed round Tel long ago, 'cause I tell you what
– you think he may be in trouble, but I don't. I
think that little twister never did anything that wasn't
right for Number One.'

'Right,' added Jamie. 'It's down to you, Mack,
what you believe.' He put on a self-righteous look.
'We thought we were helping, passing on these
stories.' Then he smiled. 'If you don't like our lies,
go and make your own up.'

What could I do? Believe all of it, none of it, or
bits. And which bits? So I decided to take the story
from the start and follow it through where it led.

were sounding off and blokes were telling lies to their families. And my glass was nearly empty. And this other bloke had pushed his way on to the bench next to me. I was squashed against the wall, so I could barely breathe in or out.

In fact, I was ready to give up. Either I'd got the wrong pub, or the wrong town, or it was just another of Tel's Tales. 'She comes in the Green Dragon every evening.'

It was Rick who started it. After I put the phone down on Lumber, I felt the need for action. So I got dressed and went round to Nick's. Rick and Jamie were there and as soon as I'd bought them another coffee, Rick said, 'Hey, we were just talking about Tel and this woman.'

'What woman?'

'She's called Glenda. She's an artist. He met her in the Green Dragon. A real mover, around forty and gasping for it – likes toy boys.'

'Pull the other,' I said.

'Look –' Rick waved his cup at me, slopping coffee – 'I do not make them up, I just pass them on. This is Tel talking. Do you want to hear?'

Why not?

'It was a month or so ago. She just came over to him. She said, "You have a fascinating face. I'd like to paint you."'

'Get away.'

'That's what the lad said. He went round to her studio, over a health shop. She did a portrait of him, then one day she said, "Darling, I'd love to paint

80

on doing something when you know it doesn't make sense – as if one half of your mind is getting behind the other and shoving it? Each time I thought it over, the only smart thing to do seemed to be – pack it in. But every time the front part of my head sorted that out, the back part got excited and I was off again.

Mind you, each move I'd made so far had brought results. But not the ones I wanted. In fact, ones I didn't want. I'd tracked down Tel's mother. I was rather chuffed with myself over that, yet it didn't show me where Tel was, it just got the police down on me. I'd followed the trail to Walkington and the army camp. I'd got inside it. And what did that get me? Nothing. But Lumber had got to join the Paras, which I thought was crazy.

Then, there was Sis. What was going on there? Who was that bloke she didn't want me to see? Why did she try and get rid of me? Instead of solving mysteries, I was just finding new ones. All I was finding out for sure was that Tel was a liar and that other people didn't always tell the truth. Everybody was hiding things. But the more I found out what I didn't want to know, the more I wanted to go on looking.

Was Lumber right? 'You're always trying to find out things but you never learn anything.' Then he had the gall to thank me for getting him into the Paras – but you're on your own when it comes to finding Tel. I owe you, Mack, but not that one.

Half-past seven. The bar was still crammed and the Damsel Lounge was still empty. The mobiles

Seventeen

I was sitting in this pub, called the Green Dragon, behind the market square, trying to make a glass of cider last while I waited for this girl – well, woman really, whom I'd never met before.

The pub had two rooms. A big public bar that went right round so you could look across the bar and see people on the other side, and a small room down a couple of steps, the Damsel Lounge, it was called. That one was empty and the public was jam-packed with the kind of people I don't usually meet, like ad men, lawyers, estate agents and computer whiz-kids, all late from the office and shouting at each other, when they weren't shouting down their mobiles.

I'd rather have sat in the lounge, but I didn't want to draw attention to myself and what I was drinking. I was sure the barman looked at me with contempt when I ordered it. So I sat in the corner with two fat blokes in blazers with crests, and their secretaries, almost on top of me. I had to keep peering round them to make sure I didn't miss her.

While I waited, I sipped my drink and let my mind run over the past couple of weeks, since I'd started this hunt for traces of Tel. What is it makes you go

he, Mack? You just want to find him to prove something. You know, you've always been the same,
always messing about trying to find things out and
never learning anything.'

He was silent, as if that great thought had exhaus-
ted him.

'That's your last word?' I asked.

'Till you come up with something sensible.'

'Oh yeah – like joining the Paras?'

'That's a for instance.'

In the end I put the phone down on him.